Murder & Menace
A Cryptic Cove Cozy Mystery - Book 2
Copyright © 2016 by KP Stafford
All rights reserved.

No part of this book may be reproduced in any form or by any electronic or mechanical means, including information storage and retrieval systems, without written permission from the author, except for the use of brief quotations in a book review.

This book is a work of fiction. The names, characters, places and incidents are products of the writer's imagination. Any resemblances to persons, living or dead, are entirely coincidental.

Published by S&S Publications

Be sure to visit KP's website and get on the reader's list so you can receive advance notifications, discounts and reader's only specials.

http://kpstafford.com

Chapter 1

I walked along the beach and watched the sunrise. It was a beautiful early spring morning. The temps had been unseasonably warm lately, so I enjoyed it. I looked up at the rocky cliffs and could see the walking path of the city park. I was trying to psych myself into climbing it. A lot of people climbed them. Kids had made pathways through the larger rocks over the years. It wasn't all that steep and had plenty of spaces to walk instead of climb. Jake and I had a bet to see who could reach the top fastest. This competition would occur in less than a week. I was here cheating, already looking for a good path to take in hopes that I could win the bet. Otherwise, I'd have to pay for dinner at Antonio's and I had no intentions of forking out that kind of cash.

Last night we held a big welcome home party for my aunt. She'd been missing for twenty-five years and we found her a few months ago, being held prisoner by a creepy mortician named Orvel Haynes, who was killed a few months back. It's been a struggle for Aunt Agatha to adjust back into normal life. She finally agreed to the party. The event took place at the city park, where I was about to make the climb up to. After all the food consumption last night, I needed a good workout.

I started up the embankment towards the city park. Baxter flew in and landed on the railing of the walk-path that was about ten feet above the only place I'd have to do any real climbing. He squawked at me. It was hard to tell if he was offering encouragement or laughing at me.

I tried to pick a path that would be easy to walk but kept finding myself in places where I had to do some climbing. I thought about back-tracking and finding another path, but I guessed an actual workout would be good for me. Close to the top, my breathing was heavy so I stopped and took a sip of water. I looked up at the large outcropping of rocks, trying to judge which way I should approach it, and noticed a small offshoot that looked like a good hand-hold towards the top. I made my way carefully through the smaller rocks, being careful where I placed my feet and hands. A good five feet or more from the big rocks I started wishing I hadn't attempted this path. I looked back down and decided this was a staircase built for giants, not for people who were less than twenty feet tall. I took in a deep breath and looked up to grab the next rock. Baxter swooped down to the ledge I was making my way towards and became fidgety. Maybe he was trying to inspire me and wish me luck. I grabbed hold and hoisted myself up over the ledge and almost fell backward when I came face to face with Will Hunter, except he didn't see me because he was dead. He was very dead. With all my strength, I pulled myself on up and leaned against a rock, staring at the dead man. This is the second time in six months I've found someone dead. My heart pounded as sadness and dread began to set in. Someone else in Cryptic Cove was dead. I put my face in my hands. Could he have fallen over the railing last night at the party?

I looked up at Baxter, "I wish you spoke English so I'd know what you were trying to tell me. Or maybe I need to learn crow-speak."

I looked back over at Will as I dug my cell phone out to call John.

Within twenty-five minutes John, some search and rescue guys, and Marcus Finche, the new county coroner, were there. The county sheriff showed up five minutes later. He stood against the railing, looking down. Most of the time he was a cold, stern man, all about the law and going by the books. A tear trickled down his cheek and his knuckles were white as he held onto the railing. He wiped his eyes, regained his composure and started walking towards me where I'd taken a seat on one of the park benches. As he walked up I told him I was sorry about Will. I had gotten to know Will better over the last few months. He was a good cop and took his job seriously. The sheriff acknowledged my condolences and then got straight to business. "So, Miss Danforth, you found the body."

I didn't like his tone, but then again, I hadn't liked him since the last investigation into the deaths of the elderly couple. I had also found their bodies. "I don't go looking for them if that's what you're implying."

"No, just seems a bit," he paused, "convenient."

"Maybe for the dead, but not for me. I'd be happy to live the rest of my life without seeing any more dead bodies."

"I'm sure you would. I may have questions for you later. You know the drill.."

I interrupted his last sentence, "I'll stay in town."

He told me I could leave so I headed home to get a shower before going into the office. It was a morning I'd dread. The phone would ring off the hook with everyone in town calling me to find out what was going on. I couldn't get the image of Will out of my head and didn't want to keep reliving it. The fall was only fifteen feet, but his face was a complete mess.

I called Peyton as soon as I got in the car to head home. They had known each other all their lives. I knew the news would be hard for her.

At nine a.m. Jake walked through the door. I had fielded most of the phone calls and could have a few minutes with him. He gave me a big hug. He knew I wasn't fond of being around dead people. He asked me if I'd heard anything more. I hadn't. I expected it'd be late morning before John came in with any news.

I fixed us both a cup of coffee and we sat down in the chairs by the window. Jake took a sip of his and then looked at me. "So, what were doing on that ledge?"

Ugh, I wanted to dodge that question. "I was practicing for Saturday."

His brows furrowed as he cocked his head sideways, "You were cheating."

I rolled my eyes at him. *Guilty!* "I was not. It was practice."

"Since you didn't practice with me or let me know, I call it cheating."

"Okay, I was cheating, but I'm a girl. Surely I get a little leeway in your rules on this?"

He leaned over and kissed me. "Uhmmmm, no."

"Meanie," I said as I stuck my tongue out at him.

He stood up, "I can't believe this happened last night at the party and none of us were aware of it."

"I know. I saw him and Alice kind of having words, or it looked like they were disagreeing. I can't believe she didn't notice he was missing."

"Maybe something came up and she thought he left to work on police business."

"I guess we'll find out sooner or later."

Jake bent over and kissed my forehead, "I have to get to work. Let me know when you find out something."

"Sure," I said as I stood up and walked over to sit behind my desk.

The bells over the door jingled about half an hour later. I looked up as John walked through the door. He had a concerned look on his face. He sat down in the chair, looked at me and shook his head.

"You have some news?"

"Yes. The preliminary report from Marcus is that Will had been in a fight before he fell."

I didn't want the answer, but I had to ask, "So, this may not be an accident."

"I'm afraid not. We'll know more after the autopsy." He stood up and headed to his inner office.

I sat there with my mind reeling. My job had been quite normal the past few months. As close to normal as this town gets anyway. Another murder case could send the people into a tizzy.

Chapter 2

I called my best friend, Peyton Lewis. She runs Cove's Peak Bed & Breakfast. When I returned to Cryptic Cove her and I picked up our friendship like we were still kids. The celebration was partially for her too. That's how Grams talked Aunt Agatha into it. Peyton's high school sweetheart had returned to Cryptic Cove. He had moved away before he knew about Paisley being his child. He never wrote to Peyton so she moved on with her life. Now he was back and she was trying to put her family together. I decided to see if she wanted to have lunch today. I knew she probably hadn't taken Will's death very well. I was disappointed when she said Mark wasn't feeling well, and she needed to stay there. My second option was to call Jake and see if he was available. He wasn't, so I grabbed a sandwich from the diner and headed to the town square where I could sit at a picnic table on the courthouse lawn. It was a nice walk and the fresh air would do me good.

Not only was this death weighing on my mind, but the fact that Peyton had grown distant from me since Mark had returned to Cryptic Cove. At first, everything was fine and he tried to get along with our friends, but then he grew more distant and it had caused her to pull back from friends as well.

I worried about her because she had lost that 'Peyton' charm in the last month. She appeared upbeat when she was working or out in public and most people wouldn't notice a difference in her, but I did.

I can't even explain how I feel. We're still best friends and still talk, but it's not the way it was. In a way, I feel like I've lost my best friend, even though she's alive and well and I see her all the time. Up until a few months ago, I didn't even have a best friend and now that this wedge had been put between us, it just really hurt.

I've tried to pinpoint what it is about Mark that I don't like. He seemed like a great guy at first and I was over-joyed for Peyton getting her family put together. But he's changed lately. He seems more demanding and controlling, which makes little sense because Peyton is a strong, independent woman. Maybe she's just trying to help him cope with being back home and trying to be a father, but there's just something about him and the way he acts that isn't right.

Paisley is very distant from him. That's understandable, all she's ever known is her mom and the town's people. Mark is a complete stranger. The fact is, though, that Paisley often opens up to new people after she's been around them a few times. She won't have anything to do with Mark. I'm sure Peyton has noticed, but talking about Mark tends to be a touchy subject some days.

I stopped by Grams' candle shop, Crystal Scents, on the way back to the office to see how she was holding up. Her shop was one of the busiest in town, not from customers, but from the gossip box. Although she did have a great business. She said Aunt Agatha hadn't taken the news very well. After living in seclusion for so long she wasn't used to dealing with life, or death. It had been hard for her to adjust. Grams was worried this could cause a setback since she was starting to come around.

She'd spent a lot of time talking to Charlie last night at the party. Charlie is shy too. He's been coming out of his shell after getting to know Jake and everyone. Aunt Agatha feels a kindred spirit with him because he grew up pretty isolated, but he's ready to get out into life and start living it. I hope he can inspire my aunt to do the same thing.

Best I could tell, the town's people hadn't caught wind that Will's death may not have been an accident. That was a good thing, but it made it hard to ask questions without sounding suspicious or like I was digging for something. One of the town busybodies mentioned she'd seen him and Alice having a riff last night at the party. Alice had gotten mad and left the party after her brother, Alan, tried to talk to her. My ears perked up. If this was going to be an investigation at some point, I needed to pay attention who all had spoken to Will last night. Not to mention that Jake had said something earlier about Will and Alice having a disagreement. Ms. Jensen, the busybody who was talking, said she'd saw Will walk off from Alice, and Alan had tried to speak to Will but he was in a hurry. After that, he said something to his sister and she stormed off. My mind kicked into overdrive. A jilted lover could be a good suspect. Alice wasn't an overly friendly person until she started dating Will, but in a moment of anger, she could have pushed him over the ledge. I didn't want to think like that, but after the last murders in this town, my mind was always trying to connect dots and figure out why people acted the way they sometimes do.

Another lady spoke up and said she's noticed "that Charlie guy," as she called him, staring at Will a good part of the night. She didn't trust him because he was so quiet and had grown up in the area but no one really knew who he was since he never came out in public or spoke to anyone until recently. She'd pretty much kept her eye on him most of the night until he walked off and headed towards the path where Will's body had been found. She looked up at Grams, "I saw him speaking to your sister too."

Grams looked at me and rolled her eyes. She turned back to the lady, "What's that have to do with anything?"

The lady smirked, "Oh nothing, I suppose. I just don't trust him. I'd hate to see Agatha take up with the young man and him end up being some crazy killer. She's had enough to deal with in her life."

"Oh, for heaven's sake," Grams said, "She's old enough to be his mother. I don't think she'll be taking up with him, as you call it. They have a lot in common the way they've both lived in seclusion most of their lives."

The lady let out a humph sound, "I still don't trust him and your sister would do well to be careful around him," she said as she got up to leave. "I have things to tend to today." She left the candle shop. The other ladies looked at each other and made little snorting sounds. Even Ms. Jensen, who was a bit on the paranoid side at times thought it was funny.

I kissed Grams on the cheek and headed back to the office to see if John had any more news. The county sheriff's car was parked out front. That was never a good sign. I wondered if we'd lose our office again like we did during the last investigation. I walked in the door and the office was quiet. I could hear them talking in John's office, their words were mumbles. I didn't want to be nosy and eavesdrop, but the coffee pot was right next to the door. Just as I finished pouring myself a cup of coffee, the door opened and startled me. A bit of coffee sloshed out onto my hand. Dangit, I cursed under my breath. That's what I get for being nosy.

The sheriff looked at me, gave a little nod and left the office. I peeked in at John. He looked up and motioned for me to come on in.

"How's he taking the death of one of his deputies?"

"Not good, I'm afraid. If it was in the line of duty, he'd probably handle it much better. Something like this puts people on edge."

"I can understand that. Has he shared any information with you?"

John sat back in his chair and rubbed his chin. "He wants us to do a good bit of the investigation if it comes to that."

"Really? Why would he do that? Does he suspect foul play?"

"We won't know the full details until Finche is done with his autopsy. That should be by tomorrow, but since Will was a deputy he doesn't want any conflict of interest issues brought up. So, we may have our work cut out for us."

"We solved the last murder case."

John's forehead creased. "You stumbled on that. And I don't want you going off by yourself snooping around this time. Your grandmother would skin me alive if I let anything happen to you."

"I still have my flashlight," I said with a small laugh.

John didn't laugh. He looked at me, "Well you stay out of creepy old houses this time."

"Yessir."

I returned to my desk. I wanted to pick up the phone and call Peyton. It was hard not sharing everything with her now. I didn't want to risk upsetting her or Mark so I skipped the phone call. I knew I'd have to drop by there sooner or later and let her know what was going on. Hopefully, Mark would be gone in the morning when I stopped by on my way to work.

Chapter 3

    Jake came by around seven that night with a sack full of groceries in his hands. He kissed me and headed to the kitchen. Sometimes our "date nights" turned into cooking sessions between him and Grams. She was teaching him the art of home cooking and he was teaching her some new tricks in the art of fine cuisine, as he called it. Grams usually did things her way, no matter what he said, and it turned out pretty darned good regardless.

    After a few minutes with Grams, he found his way into the family room where I was enjoying a nice glass of wine. He sat down, put his arm around me and asked about my day. He always knew when I needed a shoulder to lean on. He was sensitive and caring. If he wasn't careful, I was going to fall in love with him. Actually, I'm not sure I haven't already. We decided to take things slowly, though, and not rush our relationship. Sometimes he was over-protective. I knew as soon as I told him that the investigation would be turned over to us if it looked like foul play, he'd start in about me being careful. He wasn't paying Charlie to follow me around anymore, so he might not be there if I got into trouble like last time.

    I snuggled in under his arm and told him I wanted some quiet time. We could talk after dinner. There was no point to thinking about suspects until we knew for sure Will's death wasn't an accident. If it did turn into a murder investigation, I wanted to enjoy some quiet time while I could.

    Charlie arrived a little later to have dinner with us. He and Jake had become good friends, but more than that, he and Aunt Agatha got along really well too. Conversation was strained. There had been very little mention of the party or the death of Will. It's like we were all skirting around the topic.

    I remembered what the old busybody at Grams' shop had said about Charlie and my aunt. I tried to watch the two of them together without seeming obvious. Apparently, it didn't work because Jake nudged my arm and gave me a concerned look.

    After dinner, Jake and I cleaned the kitchen. We'd been non-conversational, but he finally asked me about the way I was staring at Charlie and my aunt. I let out a soft chuckle. "It's silly."

"I like silly. You're always too serious. Spill it."

I turned to face him. I could feel my face blushing. "The other day in the candle shop, one of the old ladies said something about," I paused and looked out the kitchen door to make sure no one was coming, "about Aunt Agatha and Charlie."

"So your imagination is running wild and you think they're an item or something?" Jake asked with a coy smirk on his face.

I tapped him on the arm. "Don't make fun of me. I was just trying to see if I could figure out why the old lady would think that."

"I wasn't making fun of you."

"You were!"

"Okay, maybe a little, but in case you weren't aware, Charlie has his eye on Peyton."

"Are you serious? Why haven't I noticed it?"

"Because you're too concerned with her and Mark to notice that anyone else might be interested in her."

I let the water out of the sink and wiped down the last countertop. "I know, but it doesn't seem right between them. I don't really like him."

He put his arms around me from behind and kissed my neck, "You have to let her make her own decisions. Paisley's father being back is a big deal and we need to support her and help her get through this transition."

Jake was always the voice of reason. I turned and put my arms around his neck, "There was a time I was suspicious of you too."

"True, and it's turned out alright. Don't you think?"

"Yes, it has."

He kissed me on the nose. "So, stop worrying so much."

"Like that's going to happen. Now I'm going to be thinking about Charlie getting his heart broken."

"Charlie will be fine. There's a lot more to him than this town gives him credit for."

After everyone left I fixed a cup of Chamomile tea. I was too wound up to sleep. My mind was flooded with everything. It wasn't just the death of Will, but the deal between Peyton and Mark, not being able to goof off with my best friend, the thing between my aunt and Charlie. Whatever the thing was. I was happy that she had someone to talk to, someone who had led a sheltered life. He hadn't been held prisoner, but he didn't get out around people until a few years back. The past few months he'd really started becoming a part of the community. He was super smart. I remembered Peyton telling me he was homeschooled. I didn't think Mr. Spidey was much of a genius, but Charlie was book smart like a genius. Every week he amazed us more with the stuff he knew.

    I reached over and turned out the lamp on the bedside table. I wished Charlie could be psychic and tell us what exactly had happened to Will. It would save us all a bunch of frustration.

Chapter 4

The next morning, I headed to the park. John and I were given a lot of leeway in this investigation, but the sheriff's office still kept most of the control of the case. I was getting better at snooping into things, so I decided to go look around. I didn't have any real powers of intuition or anything like that, but once in a while, I'd get a tingle that worked its way up my spine. Sometimes it panned out, sometimes it didn't.

I stood at the railing trying to work up the nerve to look down. The body wouldn't be there since it was at the coroner's office, but I'd still see the vision in my head and know that it's the place Will took his last breath.

Baxter flew in and landed on the rail. "How did you know I was here?"

He squawked and cocked his head sideways looking at me.

"I don't want to look down," I told him. "I know I have to, but it's hard."

He hopped down from the railing to the edge of the sidewalk and began pecking in the dirt.

So much for moral support from a bird, I thought. My hands gripped the railing. I felt my chest tighten and my stomach began to churn as I slowly tilted my head to look down and stared at the spot where Will's body had lain.

Jake and I were supposed to make the climb around those rocks this weekend. I wasn't sure I could bring myself to do it now. My eyes were drawn to the blood that was still on the rocks. It had been dried by yesterday's sun, but it was still visible. I don't know how long I stood there just looking at it when it occurred to me something wasn't right. I leaned forward a bit, with my hands still gripping the metal bar of the rail, and looked straight down from the side of the ledge. I looked back to where his body had been. If he had fallen he would have landed close to the rock wall, but the body had been several feet out on the ledge-like outcropping of dirt and rocks. I focused my eyes but didn't see any blood marks that looked like he'd crawled to the spot where he was found.

Baxter flapped his wings around, bringing my thoughts back to the moment. He flew up to the rail and pecked at my hand. I looked and saw something in his beak. I opened my hand as he dropped a button into my palm. "Thanks, Baxter," I said as I put the button in my pocket. I would add it to the many treasures he'd given me over the last several months. I had a collection of buttons, shiny gum wrappers, kid's toys, bottle caps and other stuff he'd *gifted* me. It was silly to keep all of those things, but it was kind of cool and amusing too. I'd often look at them and think how great it would be to be a bird and my only worry would be to collect bits of stuff people had discarded.

I kept them all because, well I wasn't sure why. Maybe I was afraid I'd hurt his feelings if I didn't keep the gifts he gave me. I patted his small head with my finger and returned to looking down at the ledge.

As I turned to walk away, I remembered my phone. Yesterday, when I climbed up this ledge and found the body, I was in shock, but I vaguely remembered taking a picture. I pulled my phone out. Surely, I didn't snap a picture of a dead guy. I checked my photo albums and found that I had. *What were you thinking? That's so tacky*, I told myself as I glanced at the picture. The coroner was right, his face was badly bruised. I looked closer and noticed a pattern in one of the bruises. Could it be from a ring? I couldn't tell on this small screen. I was sure Mr. Finche would notice something like that. Unless the morning sun had caused discoloration between the time I took the picture and they got the body to the coroner's office.

I told Baxter I was heading to the office. He chirped and flew off towards Grams' house.

Once I got to the office, I emailed the picture to myself so I could print it off. I thought it'd be good to have when I went to see Mr. Finche.

Chapter 5

The autopsy report stated that Will Hunter had died from blunt force trauma to the head. Mr. Finche acknowledged the strange bruising in the picture I showed him and agreed a ring probably caused it from someone punching him in the jaw. The odd thing was the injury that caused his death was on the back of the head, but as my picture showed and as Mr. Finche's own photos showed at the scene, Will was laying face down on the ledge. That means he had to be thrown over the railing. There was no bruising on his knuckles, so it's likely he knew his attacker and didn't have a chance to fight back before the fatal blow struck his head. Finche also found bruising between Will's fingers. If he was still alive as he fell and the fall finished him off, it was likely he hit a rock with his hand and some bruising occurred.

Once again, Cryptic Cove had a killer on the loose. The town's people were still talking about the last murders that took place here. This news would be another shocking blow to them. I knew as soon as the information was made public my phone would ring non-stop. People would call with their own suspect lists, point fingers, and the gossip would lead to at least a dozen versions of the story. Our lives would be total chaos again.

I took a copy of the autopsy report and the pictures back to the office. I knew John would want to see them and go over them with the sheriff. Just as I suspected, a few people saw me leaving the coroner's office with a file. By the time I reached the office, the phone calls started. In between fielding phone calls, we set up a whiteboard and a pin board in John's office. People only went in there on official business, so we knew it'd be safe from public view while we tried to piece things together.

A few of the callers reported they had seen Will fighting with Alice and Alan earlier in the evening. Alice isn't well-liked in this town, not as well as her brother and sister. She's not unfriendly, but she can be a bit of a drama queen, blowing things out of proportion. A few of the people believed it was a crime of passion. Those things were all over the TV shows these days. *Poor little Alice could have snapped*, some of them said. I thought it unlikely, but a few people had mentioned the argument between her and Will. I would have to question her at some point. I didn't look forward to it. According to Marcus Finche, he had unusually high amounts of some spices in his system. With Alice being a herbalist, I'd have to question her about that too. Was she trying to poison him and got tired of waiting?

I stopped by Spice & Thyme, the herbal shop ran by Alice and Annie Drake. Annie said Alice still wasn't ready to return to work, but that I could go to their home and speak with her there. It had only been 3 days since Will's death, so it was understandable she might not be ready to face the public just yet, but it could also mean she was playing the grieving girlfriend a little too long. Rumors were that they had been talking about marriage even though they'd only been dating a few months. Maybe they were deeply in love. They'd had a huge fight in public, though. I couldn't ignore that. Couples do fight and still love each other, but reports from onlookers indicated it was a pretty heated argument. Alice was known to be the jealous type. Could she be jealous enough to kill him? And who would she be jealous of? Will wasn't seeing anyone else unless it was in secret and Alice found out. I'd have to add that to my line of questions.

My job had been quite amusing the past few months. After everything settled down from the last murder in this small town, it had been relatively peaceful. The most John and I had dealt with were the occasional cat in a tree, property line disputes and who was cheating at bingo on Thursday nights. I dreaded having to ask questions about this. The town's people had gotten to know me better, but I didn't want to snoop around asking questions about someone killing the man. Many would be offended even if they understood it was my job. There was also still some tension between Alice and I. I never quite figured out what it was about. We were on speaking terms, but we'd never be best buddies or anything like that. The last time I questioned her, when the elderly couple was murdered, it was more of a research task into poisonous plants. This time, it would be a case of practically pointing a finger at her. I doubted she'd take it very well. It was something that had to be done, despite my not wanting to do it.

The Drake's owned a beautiful estate down in the valley from town. It had been in their family for years and was the perfect location for growing many of the herbs and plants they sold in their store. The housekeeper opened the large glass doors that led inside. The entrance was wide and led all the way to a set of french doors on the back side of the house. Each wall was lined with trees and plants of different varieties. It was almost like walking through a jungle. About half way to the back doors movement to my left caught my attention. I turned and came almost face to face with a large lizard. I let out a little yelp and grabbed my chest. The housekeeper turned to look at me. "I'm so sorry, I should have warned you. That's Artichoke. He belongs to Alan."

"Strange name for a lizard," I said trying to stifle a giggle.

"Alan has had him since he was a small boy. Back then it was a cute name."

"I didn't know he was into exotic animals."

The housekeeper had a look of displeasure, "The whole family is," she said as she waved her hand around in the air.

"Oh?" I wondered if I should keep my eyes out for a large snake that could squeeze me to death.

The lady opened the back door of the estate that opened to a large, pristine yard. She pointed to one area in the direction of Alice. "Thank you," I told her as I headed out across the plush grass.

Alice was sitting in a freestanding swing, curled up in a thin blanket. She barely noticed that I had walked up. She was usually well kept in her appearance, but her hair was a mess, her eyes were red from crying for days and she looked very pale. If this was all an act, she was taking it to the extreme. She finally looked at me as I sat down in one of the patio chairs. In her eyes, she had the look of a child who was frail and lost.

My heart sank seeing her in this condition. It made the questions I needed to ask even harder. I had no clue where to start or how to even open the conversation at this point. I started with the obvious, "Alice, I'm so sorry about Will."

She raised her eyes, "Thank you." Her voice was far away.

I took in a long breath trying to prepare myself for the information I needed from her. "Are you aware that his death has been ruled as intentional? It wasn't an accident."

Tears formed in her eyes, "Who would kill Will? The people here loved him." She looked down and fidgeted with her blanket before raising her eyes back to me, "They think I did it, don't they? That's why you're here."

I reached out and touched her hand, "I'm here to get answers, not to accuse you."

She pulled her hand back as something under the blanket moved, her reservations about me and why I was here being apparent. I removed my hand so I didn't disturb the pet she had in her lap and sat back in the chair.

A small head popped out and startled me. It was the strangest looking dog, oh no, it was a tiny monkey. Alice had a marmoset cuddled up with her. The monkey came out and climbed all over the swing, quietly chattering to itself. I had to admit it was the cutest thing I'd ever seen.

I collected my thoughts to the last thing she'd said, about the reason I was here. It was times like this that made me hate my job. It wasn't even my job. I was supposed to be a secretary, not an investigator or an interrogator. I pulled my notebook out and flipped to my notes. The first items I had listed pertained to the spices found in Will's system. If I mentioned those first it would surely make Alice think I was there to accuse her. I had to start somewhere, "I hate to ask, but some people have reported that you and Will were fighting the night of the party."

Alice looked away, "It seems silly now, doesn't it?"

"What, that you were fighting?"

She turned back to look at me. "Yes. I was being jealous, over nothing. I've tried to get over my insecurities. Will had helped me so much, but I had a dumb moment and my old self came out before I could stop it."

I hated to pry into people's past lives, but I found myself intrigued and wanted to know more. The gossip bug had bitten me hard. I would never share this information with anyone except John unless it turned out to be a part of the case, but I had to know. "I didn't know you had insecurity issues. That must be hard to deal with."

Alice let out a slight chuckle, "Surely the whole town knows how insecure I am., but maybe that's why they all think I'm just a spoiled rotten brat. I don't mean to be rude, it just comes out that way because I feel so unsure of myself all the time."

What she said made sense. I'd never thought of her being insecure, but what I remembered from some of my psychology classes suggested that insecurity could come out in many forms. I also remembered that people could be rude for many reasons, not just because they were unhappy or didn't like other people. "Do you know why you feel that way?" I asked.

"Not really. I've just always thought of my brother and sister as being so perfect and there's no way I could ever match up to them. I don't give people a chance to like me because I don't believe they would even like me if I gave them the chance."

"It sounds like you've thought about this in depth and maybe read up on it."

"I didn't until Will came along. He noticed it by my behavior sometimes. We used to talk for hours about this stuff." She looked straight at me, "He liked the study of human behavior. I got mad at him when we first started dating because I thought he was using me as a case study or something." She picked at the blanket in her lap. "That's how insecure I am, I guess." She took in a long breath. "Over time, he convinced me that he really did care about me." Tears started to form in her eyes, "He even fell in love with me." Those last words caused the tears to stream down her face. I couldn't stand to see her in so much agony. I grabbed a tissue and sat down beside her on the swing. I didn't care if she didn't like me. She was in pain and needed someone to comfort her. I handed her the tissue. After a few minutes, she looked up at me. "I'm sorry I'm such a mess. Please find who did this. I will share any information I can that may help you. Ask me whatever questions you need."

Her resolve had changed in a heartbeat. I wasn't sure how to take it, but I decided to ask her about the substances found in Will's bloodstream and get this part of the questioning over with. Maybe she'd be forthcoming like she said.

The little monkey had been staring at me from the top of the swing Alice was seated on. As cute as it was, it was kind of creepy to be watched by a monkey. He came down one of the posts and then jumped to my lap. I squealed and threw my hands up, unsure what to do. I had gotten used to Baxter, but I wasn't sure about this little guy. He was also startled by my sounds and jerky movements. Alice patted the seat beside her. "Wolfman, be nice to our guest. Come over here and sit."

Wolfman? The name was actually quite befitting of him as he did look like a small wolfman. He complied and hopped over to the swing to sit beside Alice. She pulled out a peanut and handed it to him.

As I was watching Wolfman shell his treat, I heard the patio door slam from the house and whirled around to see Alan heading towards us. His pace was fast. The scowl across his face told me he was not happy to see me. He started speaking about half way across the yard, "What are you doing here, bothering my sister?"

I stood up, "Hello Alan." I extended my hand, but he ignored it. "I was offering my condolences to Alice on the death of Will."

He got in my face, "That's a lie and you know it. You're here because the constable sent you to question her." He pointed to Alice.

I turned to look at Alice, she was visibly distraught over the behavior of her brother. She opened her mouth, her bottom lip quivered but no words came out. I looked back at Alan, "It seems you're the one who's upset her. She had stopped crying while I was speaking to her."

"She's crying because she's still in mourning. I think you should leave. We don't need you around here reminding her of her misery."

I grabbed my things from the seat I had been sitting in and looked at Alice, "We'll talk again soon. Thank you for your time."

Alice nodded as Alan spoke up again, "You will not be talking to her again. Leave her alone."

"Have a nice day, Alan," I said as I headed towards the house. I've never seen him act so rude or defensive. He was always pleasant to be around. His protective, brotherly instincts had kicked into over-drive I assumed, but it was completely uncalled for where I was concerned. I made it to my car and cranked the engine. I rolled down the windows as I drove through the countryside heading back to town. Maybe listening to the wind blow would clear my mind. It didn't.

Chapter 6

The discussion with Alice was interesting, to say the least. I learned a few things about the herbal treatments she'd been giving Will, but what I found the most disturbing was how she spoke to me like we were friends. She wasn't her usual snippy-self. I don't know if it was an act. If so, it was a good one. I left the Drake estate with even more questions and some concerns about another matter unrelated to Will's death. On the way back to town I stopped at the park. I stood at the overlook. The yellow police tape was now gone but I could still see traces of fingerprint powder on the railing. I thought about how senseless this was as I stared down at the beach.

I knew there was nothing I could do by hanging out at the spot where Will had died so I headed to Peyton's on my way back to the office. Something Alice said had me concerned and since I wasn't ready to answer phone calls, I thought I'd go check on my best friend. I've been concerned about Mark being back in her life. The more I'm around him the moodier he tends to be. Apparently, I'm not the only one who's noticed. Alice said Will was concerned about it too. I thought I'd try to speak about the case with her, but I also wanted to question her to see if Will had mentioned his concerns to her. I would need to be subtle. The slightest hint of concerns about Mark tended to set her off these days.

I pulled up in her driveway, behind the main part of the B&B, and glanced down at my watch. Sometimes she was working at this hour and sometimes she was in her private living quarters on the top floor. I thought I'd try upstairs first. I entered the back entrance and hit the back stairs instead of using the elevator her parents had installed a few years back.

As I approached the door to Peyton's living quarters I heard arguing. I stood at the door and listened. I couldn't make out the words but it was definitely Mark. *Crap, I was hoping he was still at work and I could talk to her alone.* I stood up straight, sucked in a breath and knocked on the door. The arguing stopped. A minute later Peyton opened the door. I could tell by the look on her face she wasn't happy. She tried to force a smile but I could already tell my timing was horrible. Although I couldn't tell if she was mad from the argument she was having or mad that I was there. I thought I saw a hint of relief cross her face. She opened the door further and motioned for me to come on in. Mark was sitting on the couch like nothing had been happening. I hoped Peyton would invite me into the kitchen for a cup of coffee. No such luck. She sat on a chair and I sat on the sofa with Mark. He barely acknowledged I was there. I spoke to him. He had a smug grin on his face and nodded his head, but didn't speak. Peyton looked at me, finally, and asked, "What's up?"

I turned my attention to her. "I've been out to speak to Alice about Will's death."

Mark fidgeted before he got up and headed to the kitchen. I knew he wasn't fond of Will, but maybe he didn't like to talk about murder, or maybe he was just mad because I interrupted their argument.

"Did you find out anything?" Peyton asked as she glanced down at her watch. Her eyes were yearning to know, but her body language indicated she wanted to rush me. She wasn't fidgety, but I could see the tenseness in her neck and shoulders. It was very unlike her to not be concerned about the town's people, but especially when one was a personal friend of hers. She was normally more relaxed, even in times of bad news. This would not be an easy conversation and with Mark looming in the other room. I couldn't flat out ask her about anything. I couldn't stand this wedge that had been shoved between us. Not speaking to her openly caused me a great deal of anguish. I don't know why she couldn't see there was a problem and that things were not right in this situation. I needed to get to the bottom of a murder case, but I was personally more concerned about Peyton's life and keeping our friendship together. It seemed to slip away more and more each time I saw her. I looked at her and couldn't see that spark she used to have. Surely, she knew it too. She had to know she wasn't being herself these days. I wanted to tell her, but with Mark so close it wasn't a good time. He was always around these days.

I looked at her, "Not a lot, just one thing that has me concerned." I glanced towards the kitchen to see if I could see Mark watching over us. "Before I get into that, why isn't Mark at work? Is everything okay?"

Peyton rolled her eyes but let out a soft sigh at the same time. "Temporary layoff. Everything will be fine. No need for you to worry."

I tried to lighten up the conversation a bit. "You're my friend, I will always worry about you, silly."

A smile almost crossed her face. I could tell her emotions were strained and she wasn't sure how to respond.

I asked Peyton if she'd heard anything from some of the locals regarding Will's death. She looked towards the kitchen and then glanced back at me. This was a touchy subject around Mark. Was he jealous of his friendship with Peyton, just like Alice? Was he not allowing Peyton to mourn the death of her friend because of his own insecurities? Or was it something else? I remembered what Alice had said about Will's concern for Peyton. She didn't have any details. That made me wonder if it was police business. He wouldn't be able to share anything like that so it had to be more than a personal concern. I made a note to go snoop around Will's apartment as soon as I got a chance. The county guys would be seriously mad at me for *"hindering"* their case or possibly tainting evidence, but I had to get to the bottom of this. Will was dead and I couldn't ask him about his concerns over Peyton. I would have to do my own investigation separate from the main investigation of his murder. If he had information I could use, I needed it.

Peyton took a deep breath and tried to put on a good act, but I could see right through it, something was wrong. "I haven't heard anything." She stood up, "This really isn't a good time. Can we talk about this later?"

I followed her lead, stood up and grabbed my things. They had been arguing when I arrived and I didn't want to make matters worse for her. I sure missed being close to her. I missed having someone to talk to about these matters. She hollered to Mark that she was seeing me out. We headed to the door as he came back into the living room. "Don't be gone long. We need to finish our little talk." He emphasized the words little talk.

After we got to the stairs and I knew we were out of hearing distance if Mark was standing outside the door trying to listen, I grabbed her arm. "Peyton, what the hell is going on?"

She kept walking down the stairs as she pulled her arm free from my hand. "There's nothing going on. Why do you ask?"

"I heard the two of you fighting."

She stopped and turned towards me, letting out a huffed sigh, "Couples fight, Lexi. Not everyone has the perfect thing going like you and Jake. You know, if you'd commit to him instead of heehawing around about having a real relationship with him, you might discover that couples have spats."

Peyton had never acted like this before. I didn't know how to respond. Her words hurt me deeply. "I know couples fight, but that one sounded pretty serious to me. And for another thing, you're not acting right.

You act like that man controls every move you make and you're afraid to speak your own mind anymore. Why is that?"

Peyton headed back up the stairs, "You can see yourself the rest of the way out."

I stood on the stairs for a long while after she disappeared around the corner. I heard the door to her living quarters close. I wanted to sneak back up the stairs and listen. Was getting caught a risk I was willing to take?

Chapter 7

Jake was cooking dinner at his house so I headed straight there after I closed the office. I didn't bother going home to change. I was mentally exhausted from the day and the fight, or whatever it was, with Peyton. Although Jake had prepared one of my favorite dishes, I sat there picking at my food. He reached over and put his hand on mine. "You had a rough day?"

I looked up at him and wanted to cry. The last few days had just been horrible and I didn't know how much more I could take. "I did." I held back the tears. I didn't want to be a blubbering idiot all evening.

Jake stood up and walked around the table. He pulled me up from the chair and embraced me. I felt my body trembling. It was nice to be wrapped in the warmth of his arms. Peyton's words flashed back to me about keeping Jake at arm's length and not having a serious relationship. I reminded myself that our relationship was good. We both decided to take it slow. It wasn't just me being a hard case or afraid of commitment. Or was it? I brushed those thoughts out of my head. Peyton was the one not acting right. I needed to get to the bottom of it before we completely lost our friendship. For now, I just wanted to feel safe and protected. Jake could be a little overprotective, but I'm starting to appreciate it, at times anyway.

After dinner, we sat on the porch swing. Jake snuggled me in under his arm as we watched the sunset. He kissed the top of the head, "Tell me about your day."

I interviewed Alice today," I said.

A slight chuckle jiggled through his body, "How did that go?"

"It went surprisingly well. She's a mess, though. Either this has hit her really hard or she's putting on a good show for everyone."

"You think she's faking it?"

"No, but you know the people of this town do, because of her history. Anyway, she mentioned Will being concerned about Peyton. They'd had an argument about it that night."

"You know how jealous she could be. She could have invented the whole thing as something to be jealous over."

I sat up and looked at him, "Do you think so?"

"We all know her a little better than we did a few months ago. You know she can be a bit of a drama queen."

"I know, but she seems genuinely distraught and like it was important to her that Will had cared for his friends the way he did. It just doesn't make sense that she'd make something up like this."

"People react differently during times of loss. You have to take that into consideration too."

"I know, but I'm also worried about Peyton. She's just not acting right."

"Give it time Lexi, she'll come back around."

He pulled me back into his arms. I sat there for a moment thinking about what Will might have known. "I think I'm going to snoop around Will's place and see if I can find out anything about what had him worried over Peyton."

Jake turned to me and shook his head. "You need to let the cops deal with that. I don't need you running off half-cocked getting into trouble or getting yourself hurt."

I pulled back, "I have a job to do helping the cops and where my best friend is concerned I'm making it my business."

"Lexi, you need to let that work itself out. Give it time. Besides, his concerns have nothing to do with this case."

I stood up, "It's concerning if he died because of it. And I've given it time and the situation is getting worse. If you're not concerned about her that's too bad. I'm going to get to the bottom of who killed Will, what he was up to and why Peyton is so out of herself." As I headed to go inside and get my things I called out over my shoulder, "I'm leaving now." I stopped in the doorway and looked back at him, "I thought you were on my side."

"I am on your side, Baby." He always called me Baby when he was being sincere, but he didn't make an effort to get up. He'd figured out awhile back that chasing me down didn't help matters. At least he still respected that boundary, even if everything else was falling apart. I walked inside and grabbed my things.

Later that night I rolled everything over in my head. If Alice was guilty, she sure was milking the grieving girlfriend part well, but there were really no other suspects that had motive. I started doodling on a piece of paper and writing the names of possible suspects. I wrote Mark's name down, mostly because I didn't like him. I looked down at the paper and saw

Alan's name. Seeing his name in print reminded me of something he'd said about Will. Was he defending his sister's honor and things got carried away? If he knew how his sister felt about Will, surely he would not want to see her distraught the way she is, but if it was an accident, he'd likely want to cover it up.

I put my paper away and snuggled down into the bed. My phone beeped just as I reached to turn the light off. It was Jake, his message was simple, *"Sweet dreams, Baby. Miss you!"*

It was our first real disagreement and it wasn't even a disagreement. It was me being upset because I didn't feel like he was on my side. I thought about Alice and her insecurities. Suddenly, I understood her need to feel validated. I replied to Jake's text and apologized before curling up with my pillow and falling asleep.

Chapter 8

The next morning, I stopped at the B&B to grab a coffee. Peyton served the best coffee and croissants in town. It had become part of my morning ritual even if she and I couldn't chat the way we used to. As soon as I opened the door I noticed she was working the front desk. I assumed her desk clerk was late or had called in sick. I smiled and waved as I made my way to the dining room for my morning fix. Breakfast was free for guests, and for me, but I always stopped at the front desk and paid for mine. I inhaled deeply before going over to pay for my stuff. I put a big smile on and spoke to Peyton as if nothing were going on. She took my money and looked up at me with sadness in her eyes. "I'm sorry about yesterday."

I could tell it strained her to get the words out. "It's okay. I understand."

She fidgeted with the pen in her hand, "I'm not sure you do. There's just so much going on right now." She waved her hands around, nonchalantly pointing upstairs, which I took to mean Mark and her new living conditions. "Plus, with Will's death on top of everything."

I wanted to reach out to her but hesitated as I saw Mark out of the corner of my eye heading towards us. "The whole town is upset over it. It's understandable." I glanced at my watch, knowing I had plenty of time to get to work, but needing an excuse to leave, "I have to get to the office early. I'll try to call you later." I looked up at Mark, who was now standing beside me. "Morning," was all I could bring myself to say. I turned and headed towards the door. I can't be sure, but I think he asked her what I was doing there. I had the crazy thought he'd seen me on the security cameras and came down to make sure I wasn't questioning Peyton. The thought of that infuriated me, but I had to laugh at myself too. Another murder investigation had me questioning everything and everyone's actions. I sat in my car a few minutes and took a few sips of coffee, hoping the hot, brown liquid would improve my mood before I got to the office.

The phones were eerily quiet when I arrived. It hadn't been released that this was an investigation, but the gossip box didn't need a reason to call up and let us know what was happening around our small community. I peeked into John's office. He was leaned over his desk reading reports. He looked up and saw me, "Morning."

"Morning, John. Any news?"

"No. I expect the sheriff anytime now," he said as he looked at his watch.

"The phones sure are quiet."

Surprise crossed John's face, "Oh yeah, I turned the ringer off. You better turn it back on." He chuckled.

As soon as I turned it on, it was ringing. The first caller wanted to know why we were late getting to work. I didn't know what to say, so I told them we'd had problems with the phone lines. It wasn't really a lie, I just didn't explain that the problem was because of John.

At eight o'clock the sheriff walked in. His face was pale and the bags under his eyes were unmistakable. He probably hadn't slept much since finding Will's body. I suddenly felt guilty because I had slept pretty well.

He walked past me without much of a hello and headed into John's office. I knew John would share the news with me, but I wished I had been invited in. Of course, my basic job is that of secretary and the sheriff still hasn't gotten over my "investigative" methods from the last murder case, but I had learned to think about things differently since then. I also wasn't quite as naive as I was back then.

Since I wasn't invited in, I let my thoughts return to seeing Peyton earlier that morning when I stopped for coffee. She was a bit more social than she had been, but I could still feel the strain between us and I wasn't sure why there was such a feeling between us. At least she had been friendly to me, that was something and told me that my best friend was still in there, under whatever hardship she was going through. That was another thing that bugged me, why didn't she feel comfortable sharing her emotions with me these days? I knew it had to be a huge adjustment having Paisley's father back, but it could be an easier transition if she'd use me as a sounding board instead of bottling everything up inside.

The front door opened bringing me back to the present moment. I looked up to see Jake's infectious smile. He was carrying coffee and a deli bag of goodies. I stood up and ran around the desk to greet him. He extended the cup of coffee towards me. I ignored it and gave him a hug. He was always there for me when I needed him and I hated that we'd disagreed the night before. I was being stupid.

After the hug, we sat in the two wing-backed chairs by the windows. He'd brought me a cappuccino. I loved plain coffee but grabbed cappuccino when things really bothered me. He handed me the bag of goodies and I peeked inside. It was Boston cream cannoli. He'd driven all the way into the city to get them for me. My heart gushed and I was pretty sure at that moment that I wanted to spend the rest of my life with him.

The door to John's office opened and the sheriff walked out. Jake stood up as a gesture of respect. The sheriff stopped and shook Jake's hand on his way out of the office, still ignoring me. Jake looked at me and said he needed to get to his office and I needed to get back to work. He motioned with a nod of his head towards John's office. I tipped up on my toes and planted a kiss on his mouth. He pulled away with a grin, "I should bring you cannoli more often if that's the reaction I'll get."

I lightly slapped him on the arm, "You should get that reaction more often without the use of bribes," I bit my bottom lip, "Although, I do like your bribes."

I entered John's office and asked what developments had occurred. He looked up from the file the sheriff had left him, "Come on in, Lexi. These are the fingerprint results."

"Anything we can use?"

"Well, there's a lot of them, one is non-conclusive, but we know most of who had been at the rail lately."

"That's good news. I'm sure our killer is on that list."

A frown crossed John's face, "Yes, and if any of these known fingerprints are the killer, this town may not recover from the news."

I swallowed hard, "You're right. I didn't think of that." We discussed how Alan had acted the day before. He agreed it was suspicious too.

Chapter 9

Not long after the sheriff left, the phone rang. Half the town had seen him come and go so they wanted to know what was going on. By lunch time, everyone knew it was now a murder investigation. It didn't matter that I had told them we weren't sure, they automatically assumed the worst. In this case, they were right.

After the phones quieted down, I flipped through some of the pages of the file the sheriff had left. The report claimed there was an appearance of someone wiping the railing of prints in one section, but plenty of prints had been found in close proximity to that part of the rail. A list of names included Alice, Will, an unknown, Alan and a print that was smudged. The unknown print was all over the remainder of the railing as was Alice's, Will's and Alan's. Back when my aunt disappeared, the whole town got a little over-protective and everyone volunteered to have their prints on file, along with the prints of their kids. That's why we had so many identifications. I looked at Alan's name and remembered how he'd ran me off when he discovered me talking to Alice. At first, I assumed he was just being the protective brother. The uneasy feeling in my gut wasn't so sure now. I made a mental note to put him at the top of my suspect list and to start digging into his past to see what kind of rift could have been between him and Will or if he was just protecting his sister's honor. Either way, I was worried about Alice. Losing her boyfriend and then finding out her brother was the reason could devastate her if Alan was the guilty party. Even questioning him could have ill effects on her mental wellbeing. My heart sank thinking about her. She was number one on the sheriff's list, but I had my doubts about her being guilty. I've been wrong before, but she didn't seem to have it in her to kill the one guy who had loved her. I also knew not to let my personal feelings get involved. A few months ago, I had suspected Jake and he ended up being completely innocent. I'd hate to repeat that mistake thinking she was innocent when she may be playing everyone and did kill Will. I needed to get more answers. Jake wasn't happy with the idea of me snooping around Will's home when I suggested it, but I was going to have to do it. The sheriff hadn't released any information on their findings if they'd even searched his house, so I would go in blind. It wasn't the first time I'd done something like that on my own.

Maybe I needed better protection than the big flashlight John had given me. Jake had been giving me some pointers on self-defense, but I wasn't sure that was enough. Did I need a gun? A chill shot through my body and I dismissed the thought. If I purchased a gun I would need training lessons on using it. Jake would probably volunteer his services, but at the same time, he may not want me to have one. He definitely wouldn't like the fact I wanted one to go snooping around in places I really had no business being.

I left the office and headed straight home to put on all black clothes. I wasn't sure why, other than I had seen it in every movie I've ever watched about robbery. I wasn't going to rob Will's place but supposed I'd blend into the darkness much easier in dark clothing.

Jake called around eight to ask about my day. I was trying to be coy. He read right through it and asked me what I was up to. I sidetracked the conversation by talking about the fingerprint results. He seemed to be content with my answer. Whew! I did not want to deal with him getting upset or trying to talk me out of what I had to do.

Will lived in a small apartment complex on the outskirts of town. Mostly single people lived there, as the rooms were small, but it was well-kept and somewhat secluded. Lucky for me, he lived in a room on the backside. I parked at the end of the row of apartments and walked down to his. It was eerily quiet and I was jumpy, to say the least. I'd never broken into anyone's place before. I had gone into the mortician's house, but since it was unlocked, I didn't have to actually break in. I'd seen people on television use a credit card or driver's license to jimmy a lock and I hoped I'd be able to do something like that. I stepped up to the door and looked around to make sure no one was watching. I slipped my driver's license in between the door and the jamb where I knew the latch would be. I wiggled it around and felt it give way. I pushed on the door and to my surprise, it unlocked. I slowly pushed the door open while holding my breath. Someone suddenly pushed me inside and the door shut behind me. I whirled around with my fists pulled up in front of my face. A stance Jake had taught me in case I ever took up boxing. A small light came on and illuminated the face. "Jake! What are you doing here?" I let out a long sigh as my heart pounded in my chest.

He whispered, "I should be asking you the same thing. Have you lost your mind?"

I dropped my fists to my sides, relieved it was him, but upset he was there. "I'm investigating," I whispered back to him.

"You're breaking and entering."

I bit my bottom lip, "Yeah, I'm doing that too. Are you going to help me or are you going to stand here wasting our time?"

Jake shook his head, turned me towards the inside of the small apartment and smacked me on the butt. "Get busy," he said, "We don't need to be in here long."

Luckily the apartments only had one window in the living room, so it was pretty safe to snoop around with nothing but our flashlights. I pulled mine out of my bag, turned it on and headed to the bedroom. I found a few file folders and looked through those.

Jake found me a few minutes later. The only thing he'd found was a couple of phone numbers on a notepad. He saved them into his phone so we could check them out later.

Chapter 10

After snooping through Will's things, I only had more questions. He had been looking into Charlie's background, that caught my attention, so I took as many pictures of the contents as I could. It should give me enough info to start with at least. Will also had one with Alan's name on it and some guy named Robert Nash. I'd opened the one on Alan. It was thin. The only thing I discovered inside was that Alan had gotten in trouble as a teenager for growing marijuana. Surely that wasn't enough to want to kill someone over, but why would Will have a file on him?

I went home that night with a head full of questions. I'd need to print the pictures I'd taken of Charlie's file, but I didn't want to disturb Grams so it'd have to wait until morning, or maybe I should do that at the office. I didn't want her to know that I was checking into Charlie's background. Grams was so happy that he was helping Aunt Agatha come out of her shell. I realized without public school records, there may not be much information to find out about him, but at least his birth certificate would help me dig into his health records.

I pulled out my laptop and started checking some of the database files I'd used when I did some skip tracing. Since I was now working for John I figured they'd come in handy, so I kept the subscription paid.

Curiosity got the best of me and I decided to check on Charlie first. Will's file mostly had surveillance pictures, which I found odd. I couldn't imagine why he'd been following Charlie, but I typed his name into the database. Several people named Charlie Matthews came up, but none were from this area. I dug into birth records of our county specifically. Charlie was around the age of twenty-four, but there were no records of his birth. I found that odd. Mr. Spidey had always kept to himself. In the search results, it asked me if I meant Charlie Matthews who'd been born some fifty years ago. I clicked the link, not expecting to find anything. My mouth fell open when I skimmed the record and found out that there was a Charles Matthews born to James and Martha Matthews. Could James be Mr. Spidey? I checked other records and found out his first name was James. How could he have a son born fifty years ago, but Charlie is only twenty-four? Something wasn't right. In the results field, there was a date of death. I clicked on it and discovered that Charlie had died soon after birth. I scratched my head. None of this made sense. As I saved the results I saw Orvel Haynes' name on the death certificate. There was no way I could ask him since the man was dead, but I could ask Marcus Finche if they still had the old records I could look at. I would definitely ask some of the older people about these records. Surely, someone would know.

I typed in Alan Drake's name and quickly found the records for him. I knew he'd been born and was still alive so I checked his police records. Sure enough, he'd been busted in high school for using the family estate to grow marijuana. I checked into his high school records and old newspaper records. It had never gone public. I pulled out my phone and looked through the pictures I'd taken of his file at Will's house. There was an old picture of Alan with his arm around another guy, both were holding up a can of soda like they were toasting something. On closer inspection, I realized the guy was Will. Apparently, he and Alan had been close at one time. What happened between them? Or were they still good friends and I'd missed seeing it? Maybe Will dating Alice had put a rift between them.

I'd been writing down questions as I dug into the research. I still had more questions than I had answers for. I knew this town had its secrets, but a lot of things just didn't add up.

My phone buzzed with Jake's goodnight text. He also informed me I was a bad liar and if I was going to snoop around anymore, I'd need to work on my skills. I let out a soft giggle. I didn't plan to do much snooping around, but he was right. If he'd been a bad guy sneaking up on me earlier, I would have never known he was behind me. I needed to start paying more attention.

I texted him back and told him I'd found some interesting stuff to tell him about. He was a better investigator than me from his insurance fraud days and had connections that I didn't. Maybe he could figure out some of this.

Chapter 11

I needed copious amounts of coffee the following morning. I wasn't used to staying up late and sneaking into people's homes. I didn't know how undercover cops did it until I remembered all the coffee and donut jokes I'd heard over the years. The door to the office opened as I poured my second cup of the morning. I turned to see Bessie Drake, a pleasant, friendly woman who seemed higher class than most of the people in Cryptic Cove. She wasn't snooty or anything like that, she just carried herself like someone with purpose and determination.

The look on her face saddened me. She was a distraught mother, and with good reason since two of her children were being questioned for murder. How was she supposed to look?

She asked to speak with John. I told her he was out for most of the day, but I'd try to help her if I could.

"Would you like a cup of coffee or tea?"

"Oh heavens, I'm already too jittery for coffee, but a cup of tea would be wonderful." She fidgeted her hands as she sat in one of the seats by the window.

I was no expert, but I made a decent cup of tea. I chose an herbal tea for her, hoping it would calm her nerves. I took it to her and sat down beside her.

"Everything is just such a mess around here. I can't believe all of this is happening again."

"You mean someone being killed in our little town?"

"Yes," her bottom lip quivered, "I think he was going to be my son-in-law."

"Really? I'd heard rumors but didn't know they were true."

"Oh yes. Will was crazy about Alice and she'd started losing some of her," she looked down at her cup of tea. "Her insecurities."

I patted her on the hand, "She had been coming around and hanging our with our bunch a little more. I could tell a difference in her too."

"I'm afraid this will set her back. Bless her heart, she's always been oversensitive and jealous about things. I tried to pay more attention to her as a child, but it's something that was deep seeded."

"What do you think caused it?"

"The death of her father. The man doted on her. She was his favorite. He tried not to show it, but Alice was the apple of the man's eye. When he died, well she never fully recovered. She's never felt like anyone loved her the way he did. I think she's always compared men to her father."

"I'm so sorry."

"I believe Will was starting to fill his place. Will was very gentle with her and showed her as much attention as he could, even though he worked long hours and all. He always made time for Alice. It was a lot of little things too. He'd text her on the nights he couldn't see her."

A tear formed in my eye as I thought about how Jake texted me every night, even if we'd had a date that night, he would text me good night wishes. I suddenly felt immense anguish for Alice's loss and pain. I couldn't imagine if something happened to Jake and I no longer received his messages every day. I decided I would go see her again. The more I found out about her, the less I believed she could kill the man she loved.

Bessie looked at me, "I didn't mean to upset you." She said as she noticed the tear in my eye.

I smiled, "I'm fine. I don't know what I'd do if I Jake. I'd never thought about it until now." I wiped my face, "But, we need to find out who did this so Alice can have some kind of closure."

"That's the other reason I came to talk to John. The sheriff has taken Alan in for questioning."

I knew they would be, but I wasn't expecting to hear the news from his mother. I wasn't sure how to reply. "It's just standard procedure. They will be questioning a lot of people during the investigation."

"I know, dear. I just don't think it's possible that Alan could do such a thing as I've heard was done to Will. He had a temper, I won't deny that, but he had more control over it than to kill someone."

"I didn't realize he had a temper. He's always been so friendly."

"Yes, he's a good person, but he is protective over his sisters. Back in high school, he beat up plenty of guys he thought weren't good enough for either of them."

"I didn't know about that." I cut my sentence off, but it seemed strange that none of the old timers around here had mentioned his temper from his younger days. I remembered the photo of him and Will together. "Were he and Will friends in high school?"

"Oh yes, they were, until..." her words trailed off.

"Did something happen?"

She took a sip of her tea, "This is good tea."

"Thank you."

She turned to look at me. "It was a long time ago. Alan had done something he shouldn't have and when he told Will, well, it didn't go over well with Will. He knew back then he wanted to be a cop and he couldn't let Alan break the law, so he stepped in and set him straight."

"Oh. Was Alan mad about it?" I didn't have to ask what it was about since I'd read the old file about Alan's little wacky weed patch he'd grown.

"He was for a long time, but after Will and Alice started seeing each other, he told Will he'd done him a big favor and kept him on the right track."

"That's good," I told her. At this point, I didn't know what else to say.

"Of course, he was still very protective over his sisters. He and Will did have words that night." She said as she turned in her seat to look me straight on, "But my kids didn't do this. Surely you know. You've gotten to know them. There's no way they could do this thing."

"We still have to check all the leads," I said. I didn't want to say anything, but six months ago no one thought Orvel Haynes could have done the things he did either. People didn't make sense sometimes. After she left, I knew I wanted to talk to Alan and to Alice again. Bessie was right, I couldn't imagine Alice doing anything like this, but I wasn't so sure about Alan having all that much control over his temper.

Chapter 12

By that afternoon John and I weren't any closer to figuring out who had killed Will, but neither was the sheriff's office. Plenty of people had motive and opportunity, although their motives weren't anything huge, but as we found out several months ago, people will do whatever it takes to keep their secrets hidden. Orvel Haynes had been parading around this town for twenty-five years, blending in and acting like a normal citizen, but he wasn't normal. He'd kept the biggest secret in Cryptic Cove's entire history.

I left the office early. Jake and I had plans with Peyton and Mark. It had been awhile since the four of us had gone out to dinner and I needed some down time. Peyton and I hadn't had much girl time lately and we wouldn't tonight either with the guys there, but it was a chance to get out and enjoy ourselves. The whole town had been on edge the past few days. Jake picked me up at seven-fifteen so we could meet up at Antonio's around eight. I always loved the ride down the cliffs to the coast. The lights glinted off the water and it had a magical look to it. Sometimes I pretended the lights were fairies dancing across the sea. I'd been so uptight when I moved back here that I'd forgotten what it was like to play make-believe and pretend. I didn't feel right about it tonight in light of everything, but sometimes the mind needs to escape reality and reset itself.

Jake was quiet for a long time before he reached over, touched my leg and asked if I wanted to talk. I told him we could talk after dinner. I didn't expect our double-date to last very long. Mark used to like hanging out with us, but the last few times it felt as if we were imposing and he showed up out of obligation. Jake hadn't really noticed and always said that Mark was tired from his job doing physical labor all day. It did make sense. The plant he worked at often put in long hours as summer grew closer. A person who isn't used to doing so much physical activity would definitely feel worn out by the end of a long day. Mark had explained he'd never worked so hard in his life, but he wanted to give his family a good life. Of course, lately, he didn't act as enthused about it. I decided to not talk about such matters tonight. He got irritated if I asked too many questions.

We settled in at Antonio's and started the evening with a glass of wine. Conversation was light, albeit strained at first. I stopped myself from talking about anything serious regarding life and things were going smoothly. About half way through the meal Peyton asked if there were any new leads on the case. I saw Mark roll his eyes but ignored it.

I shifted in my seat and chose my response well since I didn't want to discuss anything in front of Mark. He wasn't a trusted friend yet. "Well, it seems he was doing some private investigating on his own."

Peyton cocked her head sideways as her brow furrowed, "Really? Was he doing this outside of police work? That doesn't fit Will, he was always such a 'follow the rules' guy."

"I'm not sure about that, but he had several files on people he'd compiled."

"Who were the files on?"

"I don't know, they haven't let me in on that much detail yet. I just overheard them talking about it."

Jake glanced at me. He knew the sheriff's office had nothing to do with this. Jake and I had conducted our own investigation and snooped into Will's files.

Mark threw his fork onto his plate, picked up his wine glass and guzzled it down. "Can we talk about something other than a damned dead cop? I'm sick of hearing about this stupid crap."

Peyton looked over at him, confusion on her face and then she looked down at her own plate, hoping Mark hadn't seen her expression. "Yes, it's such a nice evening, let's not ruin it by talking about anything serious. I'm sorry. I know you two need a night away from work, I shouldn't have asked."

The look in her eye sent waves of empathy through my body. Peyton wasn't one to back down or let someone tell her what she could talk about. I glanced over at Mark, he was still visibly irritated. The waitress poured him another glass of wine, he downed it immediately and requested she fill it again before she could leave.

I looked back at Peyton as she pushed food around her plate with her fork. "It's okay, sweetie, but you're right, we need to enjoy the evening." I tried to lighten the conversation, "How's Paisley doing?"

Peyton visibly sucked in a breath while Mark shoveled his food into his mouth like he was in a hurry. Peyton almost smiled, but stopped herself, "She's good. She's been gone to camp. It's a special nature camp where they learn about flowers blooming, bears waking up from hibernation, stuff like that. She'll be back in two days."

"Oh, that sounds like fun. I bet she's having a good time. She has a way with animals. I bet she's tickled to learn more about their natural habits."

Peyton giggled, "As long as she's not trying to feed carrots to the bears."

I laughed out loud. "Definitely, they are a bit more dangerous than the rabbits in Grams' backyard."

Mark dropped his fork onto his plate. He'd scarfed his food down quickly. He gulped down his glass of wine and stood up. "I hate to rush everyone, but I need to get up in the morning. We need to hit the sack."

Peyton looked down at her half-eaten food. She tried to sound chipper, "Oh yes, I forgot it's an early day."

They said their goodbyes and headed out of the restaurant. Jake and I stayed to finish our meal. We both sat in silence for a few minutes, neither of us touching the remainder of food on our plates. He finally looked up at me, "I think you're right about Mark. He is acting strange, and Peyton isn't the same person she was."

I gave Jake a half smile, glad he saw it for himself, but worry filled me about Peyton. "I'm afraid he's one of those guys that will charm you until he gets in your life and then wants to control you. I know Peyton doesn't have a lot of money or anything, but she does have a nice little nest egg and a good business that will sustain her for the rest of her life. I just hope he's not after that."

"Me too," Jake said as he reached over and took my hand. "I still think you should try to stay out of it, but I understand why you've been trying to talk to her about it."

"It's really not a good time to be stirring up strife with her either, with this murder investigation and everything going on. I don't want to add to her worries and frustration."

Jake smiled, "You're a good, caring friend. Let's figure out who killed Will so you can move your focus to helping Peyton."

As bad as the evening had made me feel about my best friend, Jake always had a way to make me feel better. As soon as this killer was found and put away, I had two relationships to work on, the one with my best friend and the one I wanted to last a lifetime with Jake Donovan. I wasn't going to let this guy get away. It was time we started considering our future together. I felt butterflies flipping around in my stomach. Having a committed relationship was a big deal and while part of me wasn't ready for that, the other part was. I didn't want to risk what Peyton was going through with a shaky relationship.

Chapter 13

Jake walked me to the door of Grams' house like he always did. He stood in front of me holding both my hands, just staring into my eyes. He bent slightly to give me a soft kiss on the lips. I looked up at him, "Do you want to come in for a little while?"

He looked at his watch. "Our date night was cut short and a cup of tea sounds nice if you're offering."

I giggled, "How about some of Grams' cookies too?"

His infectious smile spread across his face. "You know, if I can't get you to marry me, I think I'm going to ask your Grams." He said as he winked at me.

Was that a proposal or was he thinking out loud? "She's been single for a long time, she might not agree to a marriage at this stage of her life." I said as I pulled him inside the doorway, "Besides, I'm not sure she has time for marriage or a relationship for that matter."

Jake let out a grunt sound, "You might want to tell John that."

I stopped dead in my tracks and whirled around to face Jake. We were still in the entry so I whispered, "What are you talking about?"

"You don't see it, do you? Just like you don't see Charlie pining away for Peyton."

I shook my head. How was I missing all of this emotional stuff and Jake was seeing it. Maybe he had special radar and could read people's feelings better than I could. "And how do you know these things? I'm not seeing it."

He led me into the kitchen, "I have a few more investigative instincts than you do?"

"You work with insurance fraud," I said with a hint of sarcasm before adding, "But maybe you should consider being sheriff or something."

He laughed, "Yeah, you'd be surprised how many couples try to run scams, and how many pretend to be a happy couple."

"Well, you didn't notice what I did about Mark and Peyton until tonight," I said as I stuck my tongue out at the back of his head.

He turned like he knew I'd stuck my tongue out and stared at me with a sly grin, "I haven't been around them in a while, remember?"

"Yeah, you have a point there. So," I paused, "What about being sheriff? You could give me inside information."

He smacked me on the butt and guided me towards the tea cabinet. "There's no way I'd give you leads. I'd spend my entire time chasing you down and keeping you out of trouble instead of chasing bad guys."

I glanced over my shoulder at him and this time, I stuck my tongue out to his face.

"See, you're already starting trouble."

After nibbling on a couple of cookies, I looked at Jake, "I found something kind of disturbing while I was researching," I turned my head to look at the door to the kitchen to make sure no one was standing there. My aunt and grandmother were probably fast asleep, but I didn't want either of them to know I'd been snooping around or that Will had a file on Charlie. Turning back to Jake I said, "I can't find any record of Charlie's birth."

A puzzled look crossed Jake's face, "Why are you looking into that?"

"Because Will had a file on him, remember?" Jake shook his head so she continued, "I thought I'd just look into his whole life and see what I found. People have known about him most of his life, but until a year or so ago, no one ever really laid eyes on him and there's no record that he exists."

Jake leaned forward, placing his elbows on the table. "Well, that's weird, but it's not all that strange. A lot of people, especially in rural areas like Cryptic Cove was years ago, didn't go to a hospital to have babies. It's likely he was born at home."

I cocked my head to the side, "You're probably right, but why wouldn't they go to a doctor and get a certificate of birth?"

Jake shrugged his shoulders, "Some people hate anything to do with doctors. There's a lot of people who have no birth or death records. It's hard to believe in the twenty-first century, but some families don't let go of their old ways."

Jake noticed I became fidgety. He reached across the table and took both my hands so I'd stop tearing my napkin to pieces, "What else is bothering you?"

I let out a long sigh, "The sheriff has a lot of questions about Charlie. I think he's a suspect and when they discover he doesn't legally exist, I'm afraid they'll go after him hard and heavy. I don't think Charlie needs that right now."

Jake squeezed my hands, "I'll talk to him in the morning. I probably shouldn't because that's interfering, but he needs to be prepared and it's best it comes from a trusted friend."

Jake was right, it would be interfering, but we'd grown to like and trust Charlie. That's not supposed to matter in investigating a murder, but Charlie was just now getting out into the world. A blow like this could cause a major setback in his life, just like it would if my aunt was hit with something major right now.

After Jake left I still couldn't sleep, too much was going through my mind. I fixed myself a cup of chamomile tea and headed out to the back patio. Staring at the night sky across the ocean always helped relax my mind. I found my Aunt Agatha sitting out there doing the same thing. I hated to disturb her, but it was a good time to ask her some questions that had been weighing on my mind, not only in regard to Charlie but on how to deal with what Peyton may be going through at the moment.

She turned as I stepped up beside her and took my hand as I bent and kissed the top of her head, "You're up late," I said as I sat in the chair next to her."

"I've developed a bit of insomnia since being back home. And I try to enjoy seeing the moon every night the skies are clear. I missed so much living," she paused, "being held in that one room. It's nice to enjoy nature again."

"How are you adjusting, is everything okay?"

"I still have days I want to crawl in a hole and hide away from the world, but it's slowly getting better. I'm still not ready to be around too many people at one time." She let out a sigh, "The party Velda threw for me last week was almost overwhelming, and then with the death of..." Her voice trailed off as a tear trickled down her cheek. She wiped it away and put on a soft smile, "Well, you know. But talking to people in small groups has helped. Charlie is helping too. He's so young and full of life."

"Yes, he is. I can't imagine how either of you lived before six months ago. I'm glad he's here to help you." I stopped talking, trying to think of how to word my next question without offending her.

Agatha turned to look at me, amusement in her eyes, "You want to know if feelings are developing between us?"

I felt my face contort, did she have that freaky mind reading thing that Grams seemed to have, or was I really thinking too loud? "Well, no not really, but since I've been working for John I find myself wanting to investigate everything."

She giggled as she reached out and touched my hand, "It's fine. I'm not quite as fragile as everyone thinks I am. Although, I suppose I'm acting fragile." She leaned forward and stared across the sea. By the look on her face, I could tell her mind was working. The silence crept up to an uncomfortable level just as she spoke again. "I had a baby."

I felt my jaw drop but tried not to act like a completely shocked idiot.

"I don't know when it was since I was never allowed to have a calendar, but I guess he'd be close to your age now. It wasn't long after Orvel kidnapped me. I'd tried to mark the days in the beginning. It was several months before I opened up to him, and more or less accepted my fate. We started 'dating' as I called it. We had an informal marriage ceremony and finally made love."

I couldn't imagine ever wanting to marry someone who had kidnapped me, much less make love to the person, but I'd read up on what they call the Stockholm Syndrome where people become attached to their captors. I wanted to let her finish telling the story in her own time but I was dying to ask questions.

She continued, "I guess it was close to two years after he had taken me that I gave birth to a little boy. He was so beautiful. I loved him instantly." Tears began to slowly form in her eyes and slide down her cheeks.

"What happened to him?"

"Orvel took him to have him checked out and get him cleaned up. It was a long time before he returned to my room. When he came in I expected him to be carrying our son, but his hands were empty. I asked him where Daniel was. I had already chosen the name, Daniel. Orvel shook his head and told me the child did not make it. There were some complications or something. It was all a blur to me."

I reached out and took her hand, tears were streaming down my face too. "I'm so sorry. I had no idea."

"I haven't told anyone yet, not even Velda. I haven't been ready to talk about it until now. Anyway, it's kind of silly, but I imagine my son would be like Charlie. Handsome, sweet and very intelligent."

I smiled, " I can understand that."

"From what he remembers of his mother, she wasn't very young when he was born but when Charlie came along she just doted all over him and tried to give him as much knowledge as she could."

"He's never talked to me about her."

"He's still struggling with opening up to people like I am. I know the town's people think it's odd, but we've both been through a lot and been very sheltered. It's actually natural that we'd find comfort in sharing things with each other that we can't share with other people. Or aren't ready to share with other people."

"Why are you sharing this with me now?"

"Because I can see that there's things you need to understand. I know your friend Peyton is starting a new relationship with someone from her past and," she gathered her words carefully, "she's not acting like she did before. I think it's very confusing for her, and for you."

"He seems to be taking control of her life. That scares me."

"I know and maybe you're scared for good reason."

"What do you mean?"

"Orvel kidnapped me and did control my environment and everything, but he was never mean or ugly about it. He truly loved me. In fact, he treated me like a queen. As hard as that is to imagine, he did. He was very sweet and catered to me. He didn't suppress my personality or try to force me into things. From what I've heard, Peyton is very much being suppressed. I don't know if he's doing it or if she's allowing him to do it, but she's not the same young woman I met when you first found me in the basement."

"You can see it too."

"Yes, I can." She patted my hand, "You stay true to her. She may need a friend before this is all over with."

I headed to bed around two in the morning. My aunt had given me a lot of insight. For someone who'd been held prisoner for so long, she was very knowledgeable about so many things, much like Charlie. I could see how they'd develop a friendship.

Chapter 14

I couldn't shake these feelings about Charlie. The cops suspected him in Will's death because he'd been seen talking to Will that night, but my gut feeling was more about his past. I decided I'd speak to Mr. Spidey first to find out why there was no record of his birth. Jake was going to talk to Charlie, but I wanted to see if we'd get the same story from both father and son. I guess I've become very untrusting of people. Of course, in the law field, that's natural. That's one of the reasons I always enjoyed bouncing ideas off Peyton, she has a trusting nature and often saw things I didn't. A tugging at my heart seeped into my chest. I took in a deep breath and shook it off. I would worry about the issue with her later, right now we needed to get some solid answers so we could figure out who killed Will and why.

Spidey didn't like cops. He wasn't an outlaw or anything like that, he just preferred to mind his own business. I never found out exactly why he didn't trust cops. He was around the age of seventy now and sometimes dislike of people sticks with you for a lifetime. Every now and then he'd let me in on a little gossip of what he saw around town. He was a general Mr. Fixit and had been his whole life. He cleaned offices, mowed grass, did odd repair jobs for Peyton at Cove's Peak, for Grams at Crystal Scents and other shops around town. Most of the townspeople liked him, although they all admitted he was a bit strange and could be a cranky old buzzard. He wasn't much for idle chit chat. Grams said as long as you told him what to fix and left him alone, he was a nice guy. He only became rude if you wanted to have a friendly chat with him. The bits of gossip he shared was normally in the form of a complaint. I'd learned if I could get him riled about something or someone, he'd start complaining and I'd glean information from it. It was sneaky, but it worked.

I found Spidey in the diner during his lunch break. As I walked in the door and spotted him, I noticed a rather foul look on his face. The new waitress did her best to make small talk with him as I walked up to his table. His voice rose as he told her to bring him his food and stop talking to him. She turned and almost ran over me. Tears could burst from her eyes any minute now. I asked her to bring me a cup of coffee and then I plopped down across from the grumpy old man. He eyed me like a hawk, "I didn't ask for company," he barked at me.

I sat my purse down beside me in the booth and looked at him, "Well, good thing for you I'm not company, this is official business."

"What kinda official business you got with me, missy?"

The waitress walked over with my cup of coffee and sat it on the table. I took a sip before returning my gaze to Spidey, "I'm not going to lie to you. The sheriff has reason to suspect Charlie in the death of Will Hunter. They'll be looking into his whole life and asking him a bunch of questions. They may even question you."

Mr. Spidey ran his hand through what little hair he had left, "That boy didn't hurt nobody. I raised him better than that. He's a good kid. Him and Will were friends."

"I know, Mr. Spidey, I just wanted to give you a heads-up. You know how the sheriff can be when he gets a suspicion stuck in his head."

He looked around the diner before he leaned in over the table. He spoke, barely above a whisper, "I appreciate it. I have an idea of who mighta done this. I'll need to speak to Charlie first, so come by the old factory this afternoon. I'll be there doing some work. We can talk then."

They'd been renovating the old shellfish factory down in the old side of town. I wasn't sure what they had planned for it, but Spidey was always hired to clean up places like that. There was some debris and old crates he'd been hired to haul away. I'd seen him pass the office several times taking the stuff to his house. He would use the wood for various projects. His last trip had taken a lot longer than I expected. It was close to time to leave the office when he passed by heading back towards the old factory. I checked my watch noting it was a quarter to five. It'd been well over an hour since he passed by the last time. His previous trips had only taken about half an hour. I figured by this time of day he probably grabbed another cup of coffee for a little boost to finish out the day. I started putting files away and shutting my computer down so I could get out there to speak with him as soon as I left the office.

I arrived at the factory right around ten after five. I spotted his old truck and noticed he'd left the driver's side door open. I pulled up beside him on the passenger side of his vehicle. As I got out of my car I glanced into the seat of his truck. It looked like he had piled a bunch of clothes in the seat. *Odd*, I thought to myself. I glanced over again to take a better look, mostly to be nosey. You can tell a lot by a person by how clean they keep their car. The pile of clothes moved and I realized it was Spidey. I tried the passenger door, but it had a big dent in it close to the truck's hood and it wouldn't come open. I ran around to his driver door. He was laying over in the seat, his head covered in blood. He'd been severely beaten and left for dead. I pulled my cell phone out and dialed nine-one-one as fast as I could. He was still breathing, but he was in bad shape. Within five minutes I heard sirens and spotted the ambulance. Movement out of the corner of my eye caught my attention. I looked up to see Charlie coming around the building. As soon as he saw the ambulance he looked towards Spidey's truck and came running over.

As soon as they had Spidey loaded up into the ambulance, Charlie climbed into the back. I noticed one of the paramedics handed him a shirt to put on because he wasn't wearing one. I hadn't taken the time to look and I shouldn't have noticed, but he had a nice physique on him. I scolded myself for even thinking such a thing as I got in my car to follow them to the hospital. I ran the earlier conversation over in my head. Spidey had information he was going to give me. Did that information have something to do with his current condition? I tried to remember who might have a grudge against him. He said he had to speak to Charlie first. Surely Charlie couldn't have done this, could he? Spidey was his father. My heart pounded in my chest. If Charlie did have something to do with Will's death, he might attack his father to keep the truth from coming out when Spidey had that talk with him that he mentioned earlier. I ran the events over in my head. Charlie wasn't wearing a shirt. Where was his shirt? Did it get covered in blood from beating his father? I'd have to tell the sheriff about it and maybe even question him about it myself. I pulled into the hospital parking lot and killed the car's engine. I took a few notes even though I was ready to get inside and see what was going on with Mr. Spidey's condition. It was going to be a long night.

Chapter 15

Jake came into the office the next morning and told me that Mr. Spidey had slipped into a coma during the night. The sheriff was in John's office. He already had a finger firmly pointed at Charlie and this would only rouse his suspicions even more. Of course, Alice was also on top of his list, but he hadn't ruled out Alan or Charlie. It was reported by several people that they'd seen Charlie talking to Will at the railing. As far as we knew, he was the last person to see Will alive. It wasn't looking good for him. The sheriff decided he had a secret crush on Alice and wanted Will out of the picture. I tried to explain to him that Charlie did have a secret crush, but it wasn't over Alice. It was over Peyton.

I lowered my voice and explained this to Jake while keeping my eye on the office door the whole time. I didn't need the sheriff walking out and hear me sharing case information with an outsider. Jake told me to meet him at the park for lunch. I agreed and he headed off to the insurance office. I was looking forward to lunch. I knew Jake had things to share with me because the only time we ate at the park was when we wanted to talk privately and not have half the town eavesdropping on us in a public diner or cafe. I sure hoped it was some good news, but the way things were going, I had my doubts that any good news or a good break in the case was going to happen.

I opened my file of notes to start running through things again, just as the door flew open and Ms. Jensen came inside. She was Grams partner at Crystal Scents and did a lot of the candle making, but her specialty was the crystals. From what I'd heard, her whole house was covered in crystals, or at least several rooms. She'd been gluing crystals to the walls her whole life and had a few rooms completely finished. Grams said it looked like stained glass murals on the walls. She was very picky who she let into her home. I'd never had the privilege, but Grams was one of the few who she'd shared her secret project with.

As the door closed behind her, she plopped her large handbag on the chair by the window and bent to open it so Tinker could come out and wander around. Tinker is her cat and he's the cutest and strangest thing I've ever seen. He's full grown, but the size of a kitten. He's solid black except for all four legs that are half white. It looks like he's walking around in socked-feet.

Tinker hopped up on my desk to get a head rub as I greeted Ms. Jensen. "What can I do for you today, Ms. Jensen?" I asked while Tinker was busy making sure I kept petting him. He didn't take to many people, but he and I had become fast friends the first time we met. He decided to crawl up my arm and perch himself on my shoulder.

Ms. Jensen sat in the chair, "I need to speak with John about this case." The words came out in a whisper like she was afraid someone would overhear her.

"He's in with the sheriff right now. Do you want to speak with the sheriff too?"

The older lady looked down at her hands as she fidgeted with her fingers. She finally looked up, "You know I don't like those county cops."

"I know, Ms. Jensen, but they are in charge of this case."

"Very well, I know I need to tell them what I saw that night. It's been eating away at me and I have to get it off my chest. I don't want to be responsible for justice not being served to the guilty party."

I perked up. Did she see who pushed Will over the railing? I picked up the phone and let John know she was waiting. He said he'd be out to get her in a few minutes.

After everyone left the office, John came out and poured himself a cup of coffee. He sat down in the chair across from my desk. His face had grown ragged the last few days. I hated to admit it but the last two murder cases had sure taken their toll on the man. There was no one to fill his shoes around here, but he needed to consider retirement. He should be fishing or something else other than trying to find deranged killers. He looked up at me, a faint smile graced his lips, "Well Ms. Jansen did see someone fighting with Will at the railing."

"Could she ID the person?"

"No, her eyesight after dark isn't what it used to be, but she did say it was someone in a dark jacket. Will grabbed the guys chest and held on to it. By that time, she was afraid she'd be seen so she headed back to the party."

"Is she sure it was a guy?"

"As sure as she could be."

"Did she know what time it was?"

John shook his head, "She was having such a good time gossiping with people from the community that she didn't pay attention. The party broke up about an hour afterward, or so she guessed."

"You'd think she would have paid more attention to someone fighting than to ignore it."

"Well, most people don't think about crime the way we do. She probably just thought it was a small scuffle and would blow over. This town is a bit lax in ways, not suspecting things can get out of hand because they never do."

"You're right and it's been enough time since the Swanson's were killed that people have eased back into their routines."

"Yep. At least we know the suspect wears a dark jacket, although I'm sure half the town wears a dark jacket."

I agreed. "I don't remember Charlie having on a jacket that night, do you?"

"No, but we still have to keep him in mind too, especially considering Spidey's condition and you knowing that he was going to talk to him about Will's death."

I shifted in my seat, "He didn't actually say that's what he was talking to Charlie about. I got the impression it was more of a secret he'd been keeping for a while when he found out that Charlie would be questioned."

"Either way, one of us has to talk to him." He said as he pointed his finger from himself to me."

I looked at my watch, "Well, Jake was going to speak to him. He thought he'd be more open to a friend. I'm supposed to meet him for lunch," I said as I stood up and grabbed my bag, "I guess I'll run to the diner for some sandwiches and then go meet him."

John stood up and headed to his office, "Let me know what you find out."

"Will do," I called over my shoulder as I opened the door and stepped out onto the sidewalk.

Chapter 16

    I met Jake at the park with a roast beef sandwich for him and a tuna salad for myself. We sat at a table with a view of the ocean. It was also the view to the railing where Will had been murdered. I found myself staring at it more than once. I couldn't believe he was dead, nor could I believe that someone wanted to kill him. This was not the big city where he had a bunch of enemies or chased down thugs so I couldn't imagine anyone having a grudge against him. Charlie was now a likely suspect. As much as I liked him, we didn't really know him. I looked over at Jake, "Did you speak to Charlie?"

    "I did. And I don't think he hurt his father."

    "What about Will?"

    Jake's brow furrowed in thought. "He didn't say too much about that, but I don't think he killed Will either. I got the impression that he knew about Will's secret investigations."

    "Will had a file on him too. That could be a motive to want to shut him up."

    "In some cases, yeah. But all Will had on him was some basic stuff. It was hardly worth killing over."

    I took a sip of water. Just because Jake was convinced didn't mean I was. "Well, I'm not convinced. He wasn't wearing a shirt at the factory. He could have removed it because he got blood on it."

    Jake let out a sigh, "I saw the blood spatter in Spidey's truck. If he'd done it, he would have had blood on his pants too. There's no way he could cause that much damage and only get blood on his shirt."

    "Well, stranger things have happened. Maybe he only got a little on his jeans and wiped it off."

    "Lexi, you're grasping at straws here."

    "Straws are all we have. The only other viable suspect is Alan. I haven't marked him off the list either."

    "Didn't you say his mother told you they were friends again?"

    "Yes, but what if that was a ploy to take suspicion off of him? She could have lied about that. Besides, his behavior was erratic the other day when I was out at their estate."

    "He could have just been protective of his sister?"

"My point exactly! How protective of his sisters is he? Would he kill for them?"

"Some brothers have that reputation, but I don't know they'd actually go through with it, especially not over something as minor as the fight he and Alice had."

"That's all true, but no one expected Orvel Haynes to be the whacko he turned out to be either."

Jake smiled, "Okay, you have a point there."

"Of course, I do. I think I have valid points against Charlie and Alan too." I had an idea and started packing up my lunch.

Jake looked at me, "What are you up to?"

"Nothing," I replied, "I just need to get back to the office and go through all my leads and stuff."

Jake stood up and walked around the table. "Why don't I believe you?"

"Because you're a skeptic. It's an investigation. You know better than anyone that we need to stay on top of things."

He reached out and pulled me into his arms, "I know that, but I also know you get crazy ideas and try to figure out things without any help."

I gave him a quick kiss on the lips, "I have help. I have you." I flashed him the sweetest smile I had.

He rolled his eyes, "Your sly smile doesn't work anymore. I see right through it."

"What? Can't I just smile at you with no ulterior motive?"

"You could, but you don't. That's one of the things that gives you away."

I'd have to remember that from now on. I was new to this being sneaky business, but I thought I was a quick study.

He leaned down and kissed me on the nose, "Promise me you're not going off to do something that will get you in trouble."

I wasn't good at hiding things from Jake. I swear the man read me like an instruction manual. I smiled up at him and promised. I knew I was telling a little fib, but I didn't need him trying to talk me out of it. And it's not like it was anything dangerous. I simply decided to go to the old factory and look around for Charlie's shirt, the one he claimed he'd spilled oil on.

After I checked in at the office I headed to the old factory. No one used it much since the only thing on the road was the factory and it'd been closed for years. I turned into the lot at the end of the road. As soon as I made my way around waist-high grass that edged the old road I looked up and saw Jake. Busted! He was leaned against his car with his arms crossed over his chest. He had a look something between Cheshire cat grin and scolding me. "Hi, Honey!" I managed to get out in a playful tone as I walked over to him.

    He shook his head, "I knew you were up to something."

    "True," I said, "But this is not dangerous. I'm just looking for a shirt." I said as I turned to head towards the factory.

    He grabbed my arm, "Spidey didn't think this place was dangerous either."

    He had a point and I hadn't thought of that. "You're here, so I'm sure I'll be fine."

    "That's not the point, Lexi. You need to start letting people know where you're going and what you're doing. If I didn't know you so well, I wouldn't be here to protect you."

    I guess I couldn't deny that I was sometimes reckless and took off on these little whims. I used to not be so impulsive, but after having my life turned upside down from the death of my parents, finding out my dead grandmother was alive, moving back to my hometown only to have it thrown into chaos, I had changed. I wasn't a great investigator or anything like that, but I had figured out a few things along the way. So, what if it was mostly by accident. I grabbed Jake's arm and headed towards the building, "You're right. You can get on to me later. Right now, we need to see if we can find that missing shirt."

    Jake followed along as we made our way around to the back of the building where Spidey and Charlie had been doing most of the cleanup. There was an old dock that went out into the inlet of a small cove. On the other side, there was a beach that no one used, and a cliff overlooking it. I wondered to myself why no one used it. It was kind of secluded and the perfect place for young couples to be alone. I noticed a white and blue boat tucked up into one of the little alcoves. It looked to be several years old and not in real good shape, but perhaps someone was using it for a little rendezvous spot. Maybe an older couple who finally got some time to themselves. I smiled to myself thinking it'd be nice if Jake and I could sneak off to the spot one day.

    This wasn't a port area, but back in the day when the plant was actually in production, smaller boats would haul the loads out to the cargo ships. The plant was used for de-heading the shellfish or something like that.

Jake was looking around behind some old equipment when he called out to me, "I found the shirt."

I ran over and pulled a plastic zipper bag out of my purse. I opened it up and told him to drop it inside. He gave me a quizzical look, "So you carry zip-lock bags around with you?"

I laughed, "Well, Mr. Finche is learning more about forensics, so I keep some with me for when I find things he can study."

"And you think he's going to find something on this shirt?"

"Well, if there's blood mixed in with the oil he should be able to."

Jake shook his head. "I'm betting he won't find blood on it."

"You don't know that. Besides, it's a good way for Mr. Finche to work on mastering his skills. I need to get this to him."

I turned and headed back towards the front to the parking area. Jake caught up with me, "Why is he studying forensics? There isn't a huge need for it in this town."

I looked over at him, "He said he's always been fascinated with it, but Mr. Haynes never would let him set up a lab. Now that he's the county coroner, he has run of the place. He also said something about keeping his brain active. It's gotta be boring working with dead people all the time."

Jake nodded his head, "So what all does he test for you?"

"Mostly non-pertinent stuff. He's gotten into fingerprinting, looking at cells and stuff under a microscope. Nothing that requires the high-priced equipment in a large lab. I think he has some of that spray stuff and a light to check for blood, though."

"Ah, so that's why you're taking this to him?" He said as he held up the bag.

"Yep. And like I said, if nothing else, it'll help him work on his new venture."

Chapter 17

I dropped the shirt off at the mortuary so Marcus Finche could do some testing on it. His face lit up to have something to work on. He said he'd take care of it after he finished up his coroner duties for the day and the results should be ready by morning.

As I left his office my phone started ringing. I looked at the caller ID. It was John. He'd finally figured out he could call me and talk to me on the thing. There hadn't been any new developments and he told me to go ahead and take off early. They'd have Charlie in first thing in the morning for some questioning. The sheriff was being compassionate for some reason and letting him sit with his father as much as he could since he'd slipped into a coma. It seemed odd that they weren't jumping to question him. Maybe he wasn't as high on the suspect list as I thought he was. Or maybe the sheriff was a kind man underneath all of that law enforcement exterior.

I decided to take my chances to go see if I could chat with Peyton. We hadn't spoken since the night we all had dinner together when Jake finally realized that Mark wasn't a nice guy. He could've been having a bad day, but he seemed to have a lot of bad days. Since he'd been laid off from his job he was around more than I liked.

I walked in and didn't see Peyton anywhere. Mark was behind the desk with the clerk. She had an uneasy look about her. Mark had a way of doing that to people so I wasn't surprised. I grabbed a coffee knowing I'd need the caffeine boost if I was going to talk to Alice and Alan before I headed home. John had told me on the phone that Alice wasn't on top of the list of suspects now. Her small size would make it near impossible for her to throw Will over the railing. Whoever had done it had done so quickly, most likely without much effort. It would have taken someone small like Alice a good bit of time to get a body of dead weight over the railing. Someone would have seen her considering the timeframe. A lot of people had been in that area the night of the party and each had reported seeing different people speaking to Will. So, it didn't add up.

I headed to the counter to pay for my coffee. I put on my best pleasant face and sucked in a deep breath before having to deal with Mark. I looked off to my right and noticed Mrs. Thompson headed towards the counter as well. She ran the local dry-cleaning service and had several garments in plastic bags. I noticed the pale blue dress she'd worn the night we went out to eat, her tan coat she always had cleaned before winter set in and another dark garment. Mrs. Thompson arrived at the front desk before I did and laid them on the counter. As I walked up she was telling Mark she came by some afternoon treats and coffee and thought she'd just deliver Peyton's cleaning. She flipped through the bags and pointed to one. "I had a time getting this jacket mended, but I think she'll be pleased with the results."

Mark nodded his head, "I'm sure she will be." For a moment, I thought I saw a smile cross his face.

"Tell her she can stop in tomorrow and take care of the bill. I know she's a busy girl." Mrs. Thompson said as she turned around and saw me. "Good afternoon, Lexi."

I barely got out a reply as she whizzed by me. The woman had a lot of energy making a beeline for the coffee area. I kind of giggled knowing she didn't need any caffeine to hype her up more. Hopefully, she'd grab a decaf.

I stepped up to the counter to find Mark scowling at me. He looked over his shoulder as the printer started printing something out and then turned back to me. "What the hell are you doing here?"

I swallowed and looked at the clerk but she simply turned and busied herself with paperwork. Apparently, she wasn't happy that he was behind the counter today. Why was he behind the counter? Maybe he was trying to learn the business so he'd have a job. I looked back at Mark and stared up into his cold eyes, "I dropped by to see Peyton." I tried to be pleasant, but I'm sure my annoyance with him was obvious. I was about to choke as his cologne wafted to my nostrils. Whatever he wore was cheap and strong. His smell was as obnoxious as his personality.

"She's gone to get the kid." He turned and pulled a sheet of paper off the printer.

Anger rose up inside me hearing him refer to Paisley as <u>the kid</u>. She was his daughter and that's the best thing he could think of to say about her. I hoped poor little Paisley never heard him refer to her as the kid, at least not in the tone of voice he'd just used. I tried to remain calm and fake pleasantness, "Oh yeah, she comes in from camp today. I bet Peyton is happy, she misses her so much when she has sleepovers at friend's homes. Having her gone for more than a week was probably torture."

Mark let out a huff and continued studying the paper he'd pulled from the printer.

I glanced down at the paper. It appeared to be some kind of financial report. I'd seen Peyton print them out each month to determine how well her business was doing. I didn't want to appear nosy so I continued my attempt at being pleasant. "I'm sure Paisley will be happy to be home too. I think this is..."

Mark cut me off by slamming his hand down on the counter. The clerk jumped and dropped the papers she had been going through.

I stood in shock for a moment before realizing I needed a quick exit before he completely showed his ass, "I guess you're having a bad day. I'll check on Peyton later when she gets back."

Mark glared at me, "No! You need to leave her alone and stay the hell out of our business." He looked down and appeared to kick a loose page over towards the girl who was squatted down trying to retrieve them all. He raised his eyes to me, "Do I make myself clear?"

"Perfectly," I replied to him and then looked at the clerk who was now standing, looking at me. "Tell Peyton I stopped by." I turned to leave when I heard Mark's voice again, "You won't tell Peyton a damn thing. Got it?"

I glanced over my shoulder to see the girl nodding her head. Anger fumed through my body. I didn't like Mark to begin with and now I was pretty sure I hated him. Bad day or not, he had no right to treat people the way he did. Whatever was on that sheet of paper must have set him off. Now I'd worry that Peyton was in financial trouble. Like I didn't have enough to worry about where she was concerned.

I pulled out of the parking lot turning right to head up over the ridge out of town. I probably wasn't in the best mood to go see Alice or Alan, but I did want to let Alice know she was no longer a suspect. Maybe that news would even please Alan. I sure wasn't in the mood to deal with another irate male today.

As I crested the top of the ridge I noticed Peyton's car sitting on the side of the road. There was no mistaking her bright yellow Thing from any other vehicle in town. I pulled in behind her and put my car in park. She got out and stood beside her car as I got out of mine and headed towards her. "Is something wrong, Peyton? Did your car break down?"

She pressed her lips together and then took in a ragged breath. "I saw your car when I left the B&B. I hoped you were headed this way so I decided to wait for you."

"What's wrong? What can I do?"

"I'd like some company to go get Paisley."

I put my arms around her neck, "Why didn't you call me instead of waiting on the side of the road."

"I don't know. Things are strange between us and I was afraid you'd say no." She pulled out of the embrace. I watched her lip quivered a bit before she continued, "I wouldn't blame you."

I put my hands on her shoulders, "Don't be silly. Let's go park my car up at Hayden's Ridge and get it off the road. I'd be happy to go with you."

Once we got on the road I decided to ask her some questions. I didn't want to argue since this was the first time she'd reached out to me in a while, but I couldn't help myself. "How's things with Mark? He was pretty upset the other night at dinner."

Peyton kept her eyes on the road. "He's just dealing with some things right now."

"That doesn't give him a right to be rude to your friends."

Peyton bit her bottom lip. "I know, but he's been through some trauma. I thought I could help him, but he does seem to be getting more distant."

"What kind of trauma?"

"He won't tell me. He just says it's some really bad stuff." She looked over at me, "Can we not talk about it? I'd like to enjoy the trip."

I read that to mean she'd like to enjoy some quiet time. I couldn't blame her for that. If he acted the way in private that I've seen him act around other people, she probably needed some peace. I decided to just sit quietly and stare at the trees as they passed by the car window. It was good to at least spend time with Peyton, even if we didn't talk about anything.

Paisley ran out and jumped into her mother's arms. It was heartwarming to see her smiling face. This was the Paisley we all loved. I could tell camp had been good for her. She bounced over and gave me a hug. I looked at her, her face beamed full of light and joy. "I take it you had a good time?"

"Oh yes. We learned about so many things. I think I want to work with animals when I grow up."

I rubbed her on top of the head, "I think that's an excellent choice. You already have a way with animals, sweetie. You're going to be a natural."

Peyton and I loaded Paisley's things into the trunk of the car as Paisley said goodbye to her new friends. I remembered how close Peyton and I were at that age. I hoped Paisley had made a life-long friend who she'd grow up with and they would do all sorts of fun things together. Part of those years were snatched from me and Peyton when my father decided to uproot us and move us to the city. I still hadn't quite forgiven him. Maybe if I understood it better I would be able to. I made a mental note to ask Grams about it. She'd skirted the topic on several occasions, but it was time I knew the truth.

Peyton shut the trunk and walked around to stand beside me. She hollered at Paisley that it was time to go. She ran over and climbed into the backseat and I got into the passenger seat. Peyton turned the car around and headed down the gravel road back towards the highway. She glanced up into the rearview mirror to look at Paisley. "What do you want for dinner, sweetie?"

"We had roasted hotdogs on sticks one that. That was pretty cool."

"That does sound like fun. I haven't done that since I was about your age. Maybe we can get your dad to build a fire in the fire pit and we can all roast hotdogs."

"He's not my dad. My dad is dead." Paisley replied in a matter-of-fact tone.

Peyton looked over at me and then glanced into the mirror again before turning her eyes towards the road. "I've explained it to you, Paisley. I lied to you to protect you."

"I know you lied, mommy, but he's not my dad."

I turned in my seat to look back at Paisley. Her face had a look of seriousness. I reached between the two front seats and touched her legs. "I know it's been tough making the adjustment, just give it some time."

Paisley cocked her head sideways, "I don't want to roast hotdogs with Mark." She returned her attention back to the book in her lap and began flipping through the pages.

I turned back in my seat and looked at Peyton. She tried to hide the look of dismay and frustration that covered her face, but I could tell she'd been dealing with this issue. The strain was apparent. I knew Peyton had changed since Mark's return and the few times I'd seen Paisley recently, her bubbly personality had been suppressed as well. I saw of glimpse of it only a few minutes earlier and now it was gone again.

For the remainder of the ride back to Cryptic Cove Peyton was quiet and reserved. At least I got to share a little bit of time with the mother and daughter team I'd come to love before they retreated back into their shells.

Chapter 18

I headed out early the next morning to go see Alice. The sheriff would have Charlie in the office around nine. I felt like I needed to let Alice know she was more or less off the hook, although we still didn't have any answers and her brother was still a suspect. I hoped it would ease her mind some to know that she wouldn't be badgered with a bunch of questioning from now on. Of course, they may still question her about her brother. I knew that would be just as hard on her.

As I pulled into the drive I spotted Alan working in the flower beds. I had hoped to speak to Alice first, but he was already headed towards my car by the time I parked and killed the engine.

I could hear him yelling before I opened the door and got out of my car. "You're not talking to my sister. She's been through enough with the sheriff and everyone else making comments behind her back. And, I told you you're not welcome here either."

I held my hands up, "I'm not here to ask her questions. I'm here to let her know she's no longer a suspect."

Alan's face softened some, but anger was still obvious in his voice. "It's about time. At least someone has come to their senses in this town."

I opened my mouth to speak, but he raised his arm and pointed down his driveway, "You can leave now."

At that moment, I noticed he had on a blue jacket and the front of it was torn. My mind raced back to Ms. Jensen telling us that Will had grabbed someone in a dark jacket. I stepped closer and stared at the torn area. "How did you tear your jacket?"

Alan looked frustrated, "What business is that of yours? I asked you to leave."

I stood straight and crossed my arms over my chest, "Actually, you told me to leave, you didn't ask and for your information, someone saw Will grab a guy in a dark jacket right before he was killed."

Surprise and confusion washed over Alan's face as he looked down at the torn spot. He pulled the material back into the place it should have been. "I lost my footing the other day and a piece of wire caught on the button and ripped it."

I looked more closely. The button was still hanging on the piece of fabric. Holy crap!

I turned and headed towards my car and called over my shoulder, "Tell Alice she won't be questioned again." I hopped in my car, hit the ignition and sped out of the driveway.

I arrived at the office just in time to hear Charlie say, "If I wanted to kill someone I would not have to beat them."

John looked up at me as I entered the office and then back to Charlie, "Explain yourself, son."

Charlie looked around at the officers. He pointed to a rather large cop and asked if he had permission to demonstrate a fight with him without being charged with assaulting an officer. The cop smiled and stepped forward as he looked to the sheriff for permission. The sheriff nodded his head so Charlie stood up and faced the deputy. Within two moves Charlie had him pinned on the floor in a position to break his neck. He quickly let the officer up, backed off and raised his hands in the air. Everyone in the room stood around with their mouths open at Charlie's mad kung fu skills. How did he learn that? Where did he learn that?

The sheriff rubbed his chin, searching his words carefully. What do you say to a guy who can kick your butt so easily? "I see," he said as he sat down across from Charlie. "Do you know who would do this to your father?"

Charlie shook his head, "No, I thought everyone in town liked him. I know our family is odd, but people seem to like him." He paused, "Is it possible it's connected to the death of Will? He was rambling on yesterday about someone not being right in this town, said he didn't belong here."

"He told you this?"

"No, I overheard him talking to the dog. As soon as he saw I was listening he got quiet and wouldn't tell me anything. Said I didn't need to worry about it, he had other secrets to tell me instead."

"What were those secrets? Did he tell you?"

"He didn't get much of a chance, he was late for a job, but he promised to tell me later. He said the whole town would be shocked."

An odd look crossed everyone's faces. The sheriff spoke up, "What do you think he meant by that?"

Charlie looked perplexed, "I don't have any idea." He hung his head, "And now I may never know."

After they released Charlie I gave the button Baxter had found to the sheriff. He wasn't happy with me, said I'd withheld evidence. I explained that Baxter was always giving me things and I didn't think anything of it. After he calmed down, he looked it over closely and thought he saw some blood on it. He and his deputies headed out the door to take the button to Mr. Finche to have it tested for blood with that Luminol solution people use on forensics shows.

I sat at my desk letting my mind drift through thoughts. Sometimes the best way to think is to try not to think of anything specific. The phone rang causing me to jump out of my skin. There were certain times of the day it didn't ring. I glanced at my watch, it was time for Wheel of Fortune and I knew everyone on the gossip train would have their eyes glued to it. I picked up the phone on the third ring. The voice on the other end was Charlie, "Hey Lexi. Don't say it's me on the phone."

"Okay," I said, "What's up?"

"I think my dad was worried about Peyton. I didn't tell the cops that because I'm not sure and don't want to point fingers, but I did hear him tell the dog something about Mark and Peyton."

I lowered my voice to a whisper, "Charlie, everyone has noticed the change in Peyton. We're all worried and as soon as this case is wrapped up, I intend to confront her."

"But what if he hurts her before this case is solved? My dad had a look I'd never seen on his face. You know he doesn't get involved in the lives of others, but he's fond of Peyton." He paused, "I am too. That's why I'm going to snoop around and see what I can find out about this guy."

The line went dead before I could protest. I didn't want to admit it, but I was relieved someone was going to keep an eye on Peyton. This case could drag out a lot longer than we'd hoped for.

Chapter 19

Jake dropped by the office on his way out of town. I told him about Charlie's skills in fighting. He looked at me with a smile, "That's why I'm trying to convince you to take classes."

"After what I saw today, I may just do that. It was cool. I've seen that stuff on TV, but it it's pretty amazing in real life."

He took both my hands and looked at me, "I'm going to see a friend with the FBI. I won't be back until this evening."

I looked up at him, "It sounds serious. What's up?"

"I'm not sure and it's probably not serious, but I've had him look into some of the names we found at Will's place."

"Maybe he can tell you something that gives us a break in this case."

"Well don't hold your breath." He said as he bent to kiss me, "And you stay out of trouble while I'm gone."

I rolled my eyes. "Since we have no leads, I'm pretty sure I won't be getting into trouble."

After Jake left I went across the street and grabbed a piece of pie for an afternoon snack. I was about half way through it when the phone rang. It was one of the gossip train ladies. She worked at the bank and while she didn't tell about people's banking business, she did like to catch up on other idle gossip.

"Hi Mrs. Dalton," I said after she identified herself. "How are you today?"

"Oh dear, I'm fine. I just called to be nosy."

I let out a soft chuckle. "Now Mrs. Dalton you know I can't tell you what's going on with the case."

"Oh, I know, I wanted to know about Peyton's vacation."

"I haven't talked to her much lately."

"Well, I shouldn't tell this, but she withdrew a hefty sum of money this morning and said they'd decided to take a family vacation. Paisley had so much fun at camp this year, they wanted to go to one of those animal attraction places." She paused, "Maybe it was Sea World or something like that."

"Paisley does love animals."

"Well, I thought it was odd to go now since her new fella, that Mark guy, isn't working."

That did sound odd, but sometimes people do things at last minute that doesn't make good financial sense. After what she'd told me yesterday about his trauma issues, I figured she probably wanted to get away for a while. A family vacation often does wonders for people who are stressed. "Maybe the company is calling him back to work soon, so they decided they should take the opportunity," I said.

"See, that's another thing, Lexi. My husband worked at the docks with him. There wasn't a layoff, he just up and quit that job."

I'd taken another bite of pie expecting her to keep jabbering. I almost choked on it when she said he'd quit his job. He told everyone he'd been laid off.

She continued to speak, "I didn't want to break it to Peyton, but she needed to know. I hope I haven't upset her."

I swallowed my pie. "I'm sure it's okay, Mrs. Dalton. He probably already told her the truth."

"If you see her today, you tell her I'm sorry for being so gossipy, especially on my job. That's no place to be getting into anyone's business."

After she hung up the phone, I picked at my pie. Why wouldn't Peyton call and tell me they were going on vacation? After yesterday I thought we were getting back on track with our friendship. I shoved the last bite of pie into my mouth, left John a note and grabbed my bag. It wouldn't hurt for the office to be locked up for a little while this time of day.

I knocked on Peyton's door. A cold chill washed down my back at the quietness. I could usually hear the TV blaring when I knocked on her door since Mark had moved in. The clerk said she was upstairs in her living quarters and I saw her car in the parking lot. She had to be there.

The door suddenly flew open. Mark reached out, grabbed my arm and yanked me inside. Peyton and Paisley were sitting on the couch next to each other, fear in their eyes.

"Look, honey, it's your nosy friend who hangs out with cops!" Mark said as he slung me into the room. He looked at me, his eyes raging and full of hate. "Go sit with your whiny friend while I decide what to do with all of you."

I sat down on the couch beside Paisley. Peyton reached over and grabbed my hand. Tears formed in her eyes as she whispered, "I'm so sorry."

"It's okay," I said, squeezing her hand.

"Would you two shut up? I'm tired of hearing the both of you and all your girl yakking garbage."

I looked up at Mark, "Just so you know, my *cop friends* know where I'm at. It won't be long before they come looking for me."

He let out a laugh. "Let them come. You won't be here."

I swallowed hard, "Where will I be?"

Mark walked over and grabbed Paisley by the arm, yanking her to her feet. "Well, we're all going for a little ride. The two of you are going to walk in front of me and the kid. It's going to look like we're headed out on our trip."

Peyton and I stood up, grabbed our purses and did as he said.

I drove us all down towards the abandoned cove. As we walked out of the woods toward the beach I saw the blue and white boat I'd seen earlier when Jake and I were at the factory across the small bay. I looked towards the factory and wished someone was there now and could see what was happening.

Mark loaded us all into the boat and informed me I'd be driving the thing for a little while. He didn't say, but I guessed once we got far enough away from shore he'd throw the three of us overboard.

Chapter 20

Mark barked out orders for everyone to sit down and shut up. I looked at him, "Why are you doing this? Why don't you just take the boat and leave? You don't need us."

He waved the gun around towards me, "That's where you're wrong. Too many people are on to me and you're all insurance."

"They're on to you about what?" As soon as I asked the question I knew the answer. "You killed Will, didn't you?"

"I did. The guy wanted to rat me out and ruin my whole plan."

"What plan is that?"

He looked at Peyton. "To get her money and head to Canada so I could be free. I should already be there, but she's a stubborn one and wouldn't buy into my happy family act like I wanted her to."

"How can you do this to your little girl? This is no way to treat your child."

"The kid ain't mine."

Peyton stood up and stared at him. "She is your child. You were the only person I had been with back then."

Mark laughed. "I guessed you were one of those goody-goody girls. I was right. I bet Mark was proud when he scored with you."

Peyton sat back down and cuddled Paisley into her arms, confusion swept over her face. She looked up him, "Who are you?"

"Names Robert Nash. I was in the pen with Mark, we were roommates and he told me all about you. He was up for parole and had planned to come back here and take you for your money himself, but I made sure that didn't happen." He turned and looked at me, "That's enough small talk, you get this thing moving or someone is getting hurt." He waved the gun towards Peyton and Paisley. I turned around and started the engine. It hummed as it came to life. I had hoped it was one of the boats with the louder engines so someone might hear it and take notice of the situation.

Paisley had been sobbing, trying to remain quiet, but the situation was too hard for her. As soon as she heard what this man had done to her real father she started crying louder. Mark jerked her up and told her to shut up. Peyton jumped up but he pushed her back down onto the seat. He turned to me and told me to get moving. The look in his eyes told me he was starting to come uncorked. He was like a madman. Paisley kept crying. He picked her up and threw her overboard as I slowly maneuvered the boat out of the little cove. He pointed the gun at Peyton and told me to get moving fast or she was next.

I stood there for a moment. I couldn't let Paisley drown and I couldn't let him shoot my best friend. Movement to my right caught my attention on the bank. Luckily Mark was facing me and didn't see the person slipping into the water. I turned, grabbed the throttle and kicked the boat into a high speed.

"Lexi, NO!" Peyton screamed as she tried to get to me, "We can't leave my baby in the water. My god!" Mark grabbed her but she was fighting for all she was worth. In one swift movement, he threw her into the bottom of the boat.

I got as far away from the bank as fast as the boat would go. He didn't need to see Charlie in the water. I knew he'd kill him and possibly Paisley too.

Peyton was sobbing hysterically. Mark became more infuriated. "My god woman, would you shut that bawling up!" He screamed at her as he popped her on the side of the head with the butt of his pistol. I cringed at the sight of seeing Peyton abused. I decided it was time to make my move. I pushed the lever down to stop the boat and turned to face Mark and Peyton. He pointed the gun at me, "What the hell are you doing?"

"I'm not going to let you do this."

"Yeah? What are you going to do about it?"

Jake had been working with me on some self-defense moves. At this point, I wished I'd taken those classes like he suggested. I wasn't very good but decided now was the real test of whether or not I could do a spin-kick properly. I pulled my hands up like I was ready to fight him.

He laughed at me. "You think those puny little fists are a match for this .357? You women in this town are stupid." He extended his arm and pointed the gun towards me. Hopefully, I was close enough to do what I needed to do.

I didn't think, I twirled around, brought my leg up and caught his outstretched arm, knocking the gun into the water. *Lucky move*, I thought to myself, as he plunged towards me and tackled me down. The blows to my face hurt like nothing I'd ever experienced. My vision turned redder with each punch.

I could hear Peyton moving around. Suddenly she yelled, "You animal!" He looked around about the time she brought the fire extinguisher down and caught him across the face with it. He fell over sideways off of me. Peyton and I both grabbed him and rolled him up over the edge of the boat.

I wobbled my way back to the steering wheel. Dizziness washed over me from the multiple times Mark had hit me in the head. As soon as my vision started to clear, I hit the lever and took off before he could climb back in the boat. I made a big sweeping circle and headed back to the shore. Peyton was in the front of the boat, scanning the water for Paisley. She turned her head toward me so I could hear her, "I don't see her Lexi. Oh, my god, she's gone."

I scanned the shoreline and saw Charlie rocking Paisley in his arms. "Charlie has her," I yelled out over the sound of the engine. "Look on the shore."

Peyton looked back at me again. I pointed in the direction of the two people on the bank. Peyton let out a sigh and pulled her hands up to her chest, relief washed over her face.

As soon I had the boat close enough, Peyton jumped out over the edge and took off towards Paisley and Charlie. "Thank god Charlie. Is she okay?" She yelled out.

Charlie shook his head yes, "She's fine, just a little shaken up."

Peyton reached them and dropped to her knees and pulled Paisley into a tight embrace. Charlie put his arms around the both of them as they cried together.

My heart was broken for what Peyton had endured lately. I looked at Charlie. He had tears in his eyes as he held onto Paisley and Peyton. He held onto them like Jake held onto me. I knew when Peyton was ready again, Charlie would be there waiting for her and her little girl.

I sat down on the sand beside them. Charlie had used his cell phone to report what was happening. I looked out into the ocean as a Coast Guard boat pulled Robert Nash out of the water. I couldn't tell if he was alive and I didn't care. He'd put my best friend through months of hell and had probably traumatized Paisley. He had shaken me to the core too. I'd never been so scared in all my life. Staring down the barrel of a gun makes you stop and think about life, what's important. Family has been the most important thing to me. Peyton is my family even if we aren't blood-related. I thought about Jake the whole time I feared for my life. It was time to let him in and stop arguing with him every time he worried about me. It felt good to have someone care so much.

Chapter 21

Two days later Grams cooked a huge dinner for everyone. Instead of a town celebration, she decided we need to have a family celebration. There was a lot to be thankful for. Cryptic Cove was on its way to being normal, whatever normal is in this town. Peyton was almost her bubbly self again. She knew the pains wouldn't go away overnight but she was thankful to be alive. There was still a sadness about her knowing that Paisley's father really was dead. She felt bad about lying to Paisley all those years and vowed to never lie to her again. Paisley was starting to open up again. She headed out to the backyard to feed the rabbits. I think they had missed her as much as everyone else in this house had. We also discovered that she'd seen the ghost of her real dad and that's how she knew Mark wasn't her father. We weren't sure if he appeared to her as a warning or maybe to make up for not being in her life, but she was a resilient little girl and we knew she'd be okay. We also hoped this would be the last time any dead people talked to her.

I watched as everyone sat around the table filling their plates with food. It was good to have a family and have them all under one roof. I watched Grams and John and wondered if he would be my new grandpa one day, but quickly pushed the thought aside. People their age didn't make a habit of getting married.

Mr. Spidey had awoken from his coma and gave Charlie some very interesting news. We were waiting on the DNA results, but it looked like Charlie was my new cousin. My first ever cousin to be exact. Mr. Spidey explained to him that Orvel Haynes had shown up on his doorstep one night, shoved a baby into his arms and swore him to secrecy. He didn't explain anything other than the mother was dead. After we all talked about it, we came to the conclusion that Charlie was the son Aunt Agatha had given birth to. She beamed with happiness and told us all that she knew there was something about Charlie the first time she met him. She finally felt whole again.

I looked around at each of the people in my life. Tears formed in my eyes and I quickly wiped them away. I reached for my glass of wine as Jake stood up and clanked the side of his glass with a fork. All eyes turned to face him. He turned and looked down at me with determination in his eyes.

He squatted down in front of me and pulled something out of his pocket. "I was waiting for the perfect moment to do this and I think this is the perfect moment," he said as he looked around at our friends and held up a ring. He looked back at me, "Will you marry me, Alexis Danforth?"

Without any hesitation, I threw my arms around his neck and cried out, "Yes! I will marry you, Jake Donovan."

<<<<>>>>

Also by KP Stafford
Cozy Mystery:
Murder and Mayhem - A Cryptic Cove Cozy Mystery (Book 1)
Murder & Mockery - A Cryptic Cove Cozy Mystery (Book 3 - coming soon)
More Coming Soon...
Cozy Mystery:
The Honeydew Queen - A Red Hat Bookstore Cozy Mystery

Other pen names:
Romance by Patti Stafford - http://amzn.to/2ECM3lr
Romantic Suspense by Ann Stafford - http://amzn.to/2FJGjWr

About the Author

KP Stafford is a Mom, Nana and Musician's wife!

She's been writing crazy bits and pieces most of her life. In 2015, she took the plunge to become a full-time fiction author.

Music is a huge part of her life. When she's not writing, she's off doing music stuff with her husband.

In a name–Vincent Price!

That's who started her on this road of wanting to be a writer—and lover of all things creepy and spooky and haunted–although she doesn't necessarily write haunted tales.

Printed in Great Britain
by Amazon